Shameful

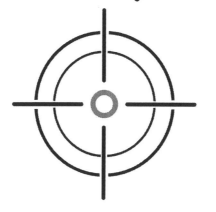

the Shameless trilogy

Shameless
Shameful
UnAshamed

Shameful

M. MALONE
NANA MALONE

Chapter One

The well of fury Lucia had been holding on to for weeks bubbled to the surface when she caught one whiff of the brunette in front of her. She tried to stay calm. Tried to push it all down. Tried to keep herself sane. But then she caught sight of Noah at the craft services table, and she lost it.

"For the love of Jesus, Mary and Joseph, Annabelle,

I've told you a dozen times not to smoke before you come to a fitting," Lucia all but screamed at the seventeen-year-old leggy giraffe in front of her.

Annabelle's eyes went wide as she teared up. "I'm so sorry. I had a rough day. I was really stressed out. I found my boyfriend with my roommate in my bed after I got home last night. And the asshole tried to pretend like it was somehow my fault."

Lucia ground her teeth. "I'm sorry your boyfriend is a roommate-screwing ass. I really am. But it is both of our jobs to keep these clothes in pristine condition."

"I know. I know. I'll try to keep it together," Annabelle sobbed.

Lucia ignored the twinge of guilt. Normally she could deal with models just fine. She didn't usually fly off the handle. When everything was going well, she was affable and nice. Funny even. The models liked her. But nothing was normal anymore. After three weeks, two days and eight hours of *Noah-I'm-A-frickin-liar Blake*, everyone was terrified of her.

And if she was telling the truth, she sort of liked the power. She liked the way people would scurry away when she walked into a room. But this simply couldn't continue. This wasn't her. She loved her job, what she did, and the people. As a kid, she'd poured over all her fashion magazines, wishing she could be part of this world. It had been her dream to work somewhere like this. She couldn't let Noah take that away from her, too.

2

Shameful

He'd already taken far too much.

With a deep breath and a silent prayer to the patron saint of would-be-murderers, Lucia sent Annabelle to scrub herself down with a washcloth. That skintight A-line dress would trap in the smoke emanating from her skin. The models knew better, and at this level they were professionals. They generally made more money than Lucia would ever see in her lifetime, *if* they took care not to piss off the bosses.

"Don't you think you were kind of hard on the kid? I mean you heard her. She had boyfriend trouble."

She turned around with a start and bumped directly into Noah's chest. "Damn it, Noah. Don't you have somewhere better to be right now? And mind your own damn business."

If this were the old Noah, he would've teased her, prodded her, and bugged her into talking to him. The old Noah was gone.

He'd killed him, just like he'd killed Lucia's brother.

Lucia had once been so sure he cared about her and that he would always take care of her. But that wasn't the real Noah at all. *This* Noah was a monster, a monster she'd had the misfortune of sleeping with.

Okay fine. Sleeping with him wasn't the problem. His lies, and deceit, and cruelty were. The misfortune didn't come from sleeping with him, because that had been— Her body flushed, softened, and warmed at the thought of Noah touching her. *So not going to go there.*

She wasn't going to think about that part. What she was going to think about was the scar on his shoulder. The scar she knew *she'd* given him when she shot him.

Lucia's stomach cramped when she thought about discovering Noah's secret. The night they both finally admitted their feelings for each other and made love. He'd carried her into the bedroom where they'd talked and snuggled. She'd lain on his shoulder, enjoying the afterglow of knowing how Noah felt about her.

And then she'd felt it, the rough, bumpy edge of a scar on his shoulder. She had never seen it before, because the first time they'd made love, it had been dark in the room. She'd been so focused on the intensity and the swirl of emotions, she hadn't noticed. He hadn't taken his shirt off until it was pitch black in the room.

But the second time, in the dimly lit room, she'd seen it and her memories had come crashing back. The chaos of that day, the chaos of that afternoon. A man with a gun, pointed at her brother. The sound of her own screaming. As the bullets rained holes in her brother's body, she'd been forced to make a decision. So she'd raised the gun her brother had given her for protection at the man who'd killed Rafe.

She wasn't a very good shot, but she'd managed to hit him in the shoulder. For years, these memories had stayed buried in her mind. But now it had all come back.

Shameful

Before he tumbled down, she'd seen the profile of the killer's face. *Noah.* All along, it was Noah. The man she loved had been responsible for ending her whole world.

The man she'd loved for so long was the same one who had ruined her life.

Now, she was stuck with him because her life was supposedly in danger. From who or what, no one seemed to know. She didn't have all the answers and she didn't know the whole story, because no one would tell her. She'd even gone to her grandmother in the hopes of getting some help.

She wanted to go to the police, to get justice for Rafe, but Nonna had sided with Noah. All she'd told Lucia was that there were things she didn't understand. What the hell was that supposed to mean? She understood perfectly well. The man she thought she loved had betrayed her and then lied about it for years.

Lucia was surrounded by betrayal. Now there was no shaking Noah. Lucia knew her life was in danger. It was true, but her grandmother refused to go to the FBI with her. And as Lucia had no proof, there wasn't anything that could be done. She was stuck with Noah; a man she didn't trust; a man who lied to her for years. The man she'd thought she loved.

"You can give me that sourpuss expression all you want, I'm not leaving you."

She whipped around to glare at him. "You have a whole team. You can't send one of the others?"

He shrugged, "Sorry, princess. My guys have actual work to do. Looping you into protection detail actually puts strain on them."

"Oh, I have an idea. Why don't you stop?"

Noah took a step forward, crowding her. She had no choice but to take a step back. When he didn't stop, she backed straight into a wall. With Noah looming over her, his heat enveloped her. She made the mistake of inhaling deep. The scent of sandalwood and something spicy injected her bloodstream with lust.

Bad idea.

She immediately started remembering everything about him that she was trying to forget. The tenderness of how she felt in his arms. The way he whispered her name softly when they made love. The way he held her tight, his hands tracing over every inch of her skin. She whimpered.

He leaned close and whispered, "Because I'm not going to let anything happen to you." He straightened and took a deliberate step away from her before adding, "You can be rid of me when we get back to your apartment."

"I can't wait," she ground out.

Every cell in her body hated him. Loathed him even. *Liar*. She should hate him. But she didn't. She loved him. Still. Even knowing what he had done. That he'd betrayed Rafe, betrayed her, and betrayed her whole family. God, the lies he'd fed her over the years. So many lies.

But despite that, she still freaking loved him. And she missed him with a bone-deep ache. The kind that had her crying herself to sleep every night. She wished she could pretend it was the sex she missed. The comfort of his body. No. It was his laugh and his teasing. And the way he always made her feel safe.

Before that night, she'd never had any reason to fear him. But once she'd touched that scar, pulled the layers back on his secrets, she knew the truth. He was that thing that went bump in the night. He was her worst nightmare. And there was no coming back from that knowledge.

Noah tossed his hands up in the air. "Lucia, I hope you know we can do this forever as far as I'm concerned. No way am I letting anything happen to you. So, I know you're mad and you have a right to be, but you need to understand your safety supersedes everything else. You don't like it? Tough. But I'm here to stay."

She glared up at him. There had to be another way because if she spent another day in Noah Blake's company, *she* was going to turn into the murderer.

Noah led the way into Lucia's apartment building. As she scowled at him, he bit back irritation and pushed down his guilt. After all, she had a point. She had every reason to hate him. Noah just wished it didn't hurt so much.

Anytime she glared at him or purposely avoided his touch, he was reminded of what he was. *Who* he was. There was no changing that now. All he could do was try and keep her safe. He'd been foolish to wish for more. Completely insane to think that she could love him.

Immediately the hair on the back of Noah's neck stood up. Something was off. The camera he had placed directly in front of the elevator was turned to the side as if someone had very deliberately pointed it that way. He put a hand on Lucia's elbow to stop her. She glared down at it.

"Can you relax? Stay behind me, be quiet, and take off those damn shoes."

"Why would I take off my shoes?" she hissed.

He shot her a glance as he pulled his gun out of his holster. "Because you can't run in those heels."

Her eyes widened, but she did what she was told. She shoved them into her purse and then cleverly slung her purse across her body.

Smart girl. She'd be able to move quicker that way.

He had to fight the urge to run, the urgency to get her to the safety of her apartment. Instead, he deliberately slowed the pace. As they turned the corner, he noted the other camera next to the stairwell. It was also turned up.

Why the hell hadn't Ryan reported that?

It wasn't until they rounded the next corner to the right that he saw why. Ryan was slumped forward in his seat next to Lucia's door. Either asleep—or worse. And from the looks of it, it seemed much, much worse. Like he'd been bent and broken and put like that.

Lucia took one look at Ryan and ignored Noah's warnings. She tried to sprint ahead but Noah reached out and grabbed her wrist, halting her. He shook his head.

"But he's hurt!"

"Look at him, Lucia. Can you see his face?"

"No."

"So, how do you know it's him?"

Her beautiful face twisted with worry, then she did exactly as he wanted and shifted behind him. Noah approached cautiously. As they got closer, he saw the ring that Ryan wore on his middle finger. It was simple and silver. Noah was one of the few people who knew the ring's significance. Ryan never took it off.

Noah crouched beside the kid, checking his pulse. There was one, but weak. He'd been knocked out. He lifted his plain black shades and saw the contusions around Ryan's eye. To top it all off, blood was running out of Ryan's nose onto his dark suit. Lucia handed him several napkins and Noah did what he could to plug the leak. Then he noticed Lucia's door was ajar.

"I need you to stay here." He bent to his ankle holster and gave Lucia a gun. "Can you use this?"

She tilted her head and glared up at him. "You have a scar on your shoulder that proves I can."

Noah gritted his teeth. "Point-and-shoot at anyone that comes out of that door that isn't me. Hell, if you have to, shoot me too. Just make sure you put holes in whoever it is. While you're waiting, call Matthias and send out an S.O.S. We're going to need some transport. I won't be able to carry Ryan all the way back to my car. They're better off picking us up out front. Watch your back. Do you understand?"

She nodded. Even as she swallowed hard, he saw her lift her jaw and square her shoulders. She was scared but she wasn't crumbling. She didn't ask inane questions, scream, or worse, cry. His respect for her shot through the roof. But he didn't have time to think about that. Without sparing her a second glance, he slipped into her apartment.

It was dark, but there was someone here. Noah could *feel* him. He couldn't explain it, but he knew he wasn't alone in the apartment. The real question was, where was this asshole?

He didn't have to wait long for an answer, because the moment he stepped into Lucia's living room, something shifted on his left. Noah narrowly missed being hit by one of Lucia's Dana Decker candles. Suddenly the intruder crashed it into the left wall of the kitchen, leaving a dent in the drywall as he tried to brain Noah with it.

Noah wasted no time, rotating on the ball of his foot and throwing a punch that landed with satisfying efficiency. *Crunch*. Instead of crouching, howling, or even muttering a curse word, the fucker remained silent. His head snapped backward then slid back into place as if Noah hadn't even landed one. This was no average burglar; this guy was a pro.

Shameful

They circled each other in the living room like caged lions seeking a time advantage. Then it was on. His assailant applied a series of roundhouse kicks, and Noah caught one to the ribs.

Shit. That hurt, though it was probably not broken. He kept his vision on the guy.

The intruder was nearly his height. Being several inches over six feet, Noah was used to towering over most people, but this guy was just as big so the advantage of his reach was nullified. For anything truly worthwhile, Noah had to get up close and way too personal for comfort.

Throwing a series of combination kicks and punches and having only one or two land, he ducked the kicks and throws sent his way. He fought for Lucia. No way was he letting this guy hurt her.

Noah took one step in and came up with his right elbow, hitting the guy's chin. This one was the hardest punch of all, landing the unwelcome guest on Lucia's end tables, covering him in shards of broken wood.

Noah pressed his advantage as his assailant lay on the floor. Even as he approached, the guy had his head up, swiveling, following Noah's movements. As Noah approached, the guy shoved out a kick that landed high on Noah's thigh. The move was familiar to him as if the other fighter wanted to injure him, but not kill him.

The move was practiced and skilled enough that Noah knew he would be sporting a bruise for the next week or so. Although, the guy hadn't hit him in the knee. Noah would have never recovered from something like that.

Noah didn't have the same compulsion to preserve the other guy's life. He was here to hurt Lucia, which meant Noah had no qualms about killing him. He grabbed his foot, and the assailant kicked with the foot in Noah's hand while sweeping Noah off his feet with the other one. Noah had no choice; he landed on his ass but was back up in a second, as was his assailant.

They were like mirror images of each other. As one pushed his hands to the left, the other pushed his hands to the right.

This guy seemed to have had karate or jujitsu training. Given his kicks, tae kwon do, too. For what felt like another hour but was most likely mere minutes, they exchanged elbows and fists as they grappled, both trying to get the other to the ground to submit.

Hell, this is almost fun. All Noah wanted in the end was to pull the mask off.

If this guy was ORUS, that explained why he was trying to preserve Noah's life.

"You don't have to do this. Just leave."

The guy landed an elbow that jarred Noah so hard he could hear his teeth rattling in his mouth. That was all that was needed to roll him onto his back with an arm bar across his neck. Noah turned his head to alleviate the pressure on his trachea, but all the while, he threw punches. Planting his heels, he tried to use his hips to buck the jackhole off of him.

But suddenly there was a crash, and the guy was no longer raining fists on his face. He was trying to shake something off of the back of his neck. Noah risked injury to his trachea and turned his head. And sheer horror slashed through him.

Lucia.

Why the hell can't she ever listen?

Even though he was pissed at her, Noah still used her distraction to his advantage. As she tried to wrap her arm around the other guy's neck, he used the opportunity to land hard fists in his face. That was all the advantage he needed. With Lucia choking the guy from behind and him using the leverage to push the dude off and jump back to his feet, they had him dead to rights. But then the guy twisted, shoving Lucia backward onto the couch. She landed with a hard bounce and a curse. The guy turned his attention back to Noah and pulled him in with two hands around the back of his neck. Noah knew he intended to hit him straight in the gut. He knew where that knee was going. But instead of using his knee, the guy extended his foot, and sent it straight for the family jewels.

Mother. Fucker.

Brutal, sharp, electrifying pain took over Noah's world. Bright lights shone behind his eyes, and he struggled to keep it together. Scrambling for his discarded weapon on the floor, he fired, grateful he'd thought to put on the silencer.

The guy darted glances between Noah and Lucia, attempted to go for her, but Noah wasn't having that and he raised the gun again. Instead of going out the front door as Noah would've assumed, the guy jumped directly out of the open living room window. *What the*— Noah scrambled to his knees, his balls screaming at him to stop whatever the fuck he was doing and just lie down.

He was used to pain. What he was feeling now was nothing in comparison to what he would feel if he lost her. He forced himself to stand and staggered to the window. He looked around first but saw nothing. It was only when he looked straight down that he saw the guy clinging to a rope, rappelling down. So he'd had a plan for escape. He had likely been here earlier setting up that hook, planning his escape.

But why mess with the cameras? And when? Fuck, unless he'd been there before scouting. It was probably because he knew he would have to take out whoever was outside. There's no way the security alarm wouldn't have gone off and no way Ryan wouldn't have heard him rumbling around in here.

Ian was right. Someone was trying to hurt her.

Lucia ran to him. "Noah, oh my God. Are you okay?"

He wanted to lean into her caress, wanted to wrap her in his arms and hold her there, never letting her go, but he couldn't. It was too dangerous.

Shameful

"What part of stay outside and guard Ryan did you not understand? Everyone has a job. I gave you yours. Next time, don't come in."

She stared up at him, bottom lip quivering. "I just saved your ass."

"You had a job. You failed it. What if he had a second guy out there and Ryan's dead now?"

Horror crossed her expression and she glanced toward the door. "Oh my God. I just heard the fight in here. And I wanted to—"

"You have three minutes. Grab anything you think you'll need for at least the next two weeks. It's time to go. We're going to my place. We've already been here too long."

He didn't want to hear her apologize. He didn't want to hear her say that she worried about him, because those words would soften his stance. Being soft, caring about her too much, would get them both killed.

Chapter Two

Exhaustion warred with nerves as Lucia threw clothes hurriedly into a duffel bag. Later she'd no doubt be annoyed by the jumble of clothes but at the moment the only thing she cared about was getting out of there. Even with Noah watching her from the hallway, she felt exposed. Vulnerable.

Someone had been inside her home. Touching her

stuff. Waiting for her. Waiting to kill her. For what? What had she ever done to anyone?

Her breath caught as she imagined this nameless, faceless man walking around her room, touching her things. Would he have waited in here until she was going to bed? Perhaps stayed hidden until she undressed? Or even waited until she was asleep? The possibilities were endless and each more terrifying than the last. If it hadn't been for Noah's dogged insistence on not leaving her alone, she would have been completely at this unknown man's mercy.

That was also something she'd have to contemplate later. All this time she'd been so annoyed by Noah's overprotectiveness and had assumed it was just because he enjoyed tormenting her. But clearly he knew something she didn't.

"Lucia, you have to move. Come on, baby."

She blinked in surprise. She stood frozen in place holding a damn T-shirt. What the hell was wrong with her? She couldn't move. Before she knew it, her body was shaking and tears were streaming down her face.

Noah dragged her to him. "Lulu, baby, I'm sorry. I am. This sucks. The whole thing is shitty. But I am going to protect you. I know you don't believe me right now, but you're safe with me. I will die before I let anything happen to you. Do you believe me?"

Dragging in the wracking sobs, she lifted her gaze to meet his. She must be losing her mind, because in that moment, she believed him. He would give his life to keep her safe. "I believe you."

"Good. Now, that's all we have time for. Let's go." Noah zipped up the bag and threw it over his shoulder. "Come on."

She didn't argue, just dropped the handful of T-shirts she hadn't had the chance to pack on the bed and followed him out. Noah's eyes never stopped moving as they walked back through the living room and she had no doubt that he was completely on guard for anything that might happen.

She didn't have to know a lot about security to be aware that staying here any longer than necessary was a bad idea. Not to mention that they needed to get help for Ryan.

Her heart squeezed as she remembered how he'd looked, all bruised and bent. Poor Ryan. She didn't know him well but he'd always been nice to her. He wasn't much older than she was and had a gentle smile.

Like the others, he moved like a guy who was comfortable in his body and very likely was a badass. He didn't deserve what had happened to him. He'd just been looking out for her. Hopefully his wounds looked worse than they were. Lucia swallowed, knowing that was unlikely. He'd looked pretty bad.

When they emerged from the apartment, she immediately saw Jonas talking to the EMTs who had already lifted Ryan onto a stretcher. Noah held up a hand and she halted. He whispered something to Jonas and then clapped him on the shoulder.

"I got this, man. I'll see you at the loft later." Jonas nodded to her gravely as they passed. "You all right, Lucia?"

"Yep. You know, just a normal day. A homicidal maniac tries to kill me and my friends."

He winced imperceptibly. "We'll get him, Lucia. And then me and the guys will take turns holding him down while Noah makes him less of a man."

She gave him a wan smile then followed blindly as Noah led her downstairs. She vaguely catalogued the heavy weight of his arm around her shoulders and the gentle squeeze of his hand as he helped her into the Range Rover. It was like she was moving through quicksand; all her limbs felt awkward and too heavy to lift. Seeing her trouble, Noah grasped her by the waist and lifted her into the seat. He glanced at her tentatively, probably expecting her to be annoyed that he hadn't asked permission.

Under any other circumstances, Lucia would have found it amusing. Today, however, she was just grateful he was there. For once, his overbearing attitude was actually comforting. It was a relief not to be responsible for anything and to allow him to handle it all. When she didn't say anything his frown deepened but he didn't speak until after they were on the road.

"You're very quiet." Noah slid his gaze over to her.

"I've never had anyone try to kill me before. I popped my almost-killed cherry, so there's that."

Noah glanced over at her sharply and she bit her lip. It wasn't his fault, but she wished there was someone to blame. She needed a scapegoat right about now. Anything to avoid thinking about how her own actions had led to this moment.

"I'm sorry." She shook herself. "I shouldn't—"

Noah shook his head. "You don't have to apologize."

"Yes, I do. I'm being so bitchy, and for the first time ever, you don't deserve that. You're being really nice to me and I don't know what to do with that."

His smile made her feel a little better but he didn't offer any other reassurances. Probably because there were none to be had. They had no idea who had broken into her place and until Jonas reported back, they couldn't be sure that Ryan would recover. She kept her eyes on the road, watching all the streets speed by, until they took yet another turn and she realized they weren't going to his office after all.

"So where are we going?"

Noah glanced over at her briefly. "The office. But I have to make sure we don't have a tail first."

Lucia glanced behind them. "I don't see anyone."

"And if they're good, you won't see them."

It wasn't that late yet so there were still plenty of other cars on the road. How could he even tell if someone was following them? What about when she had to go to work tomorrow? There was no way she could miss it. It was

Shameful

Adriana's first show and they'd been working on this all year. But was she going to be safe? Was she endangering everyone else there by attending?

"What do I do, Noah? I have to go to work. I have a life." She turned to watch his profile as he drove, struck as always by how fierce he looked. Then something occurred to her and she gasped. "Oh my God. *Nonna*. You have to check on Nonna. P-p-put her in protective custody or something. That psycho could be after her too."

Noah reached over and grabbed her hand. "She's fine. I've had a friend watching her for years. I texted him while you were packing and there's been nothing out of the ordinary tonight."

"Thank God." Lucia sagged against the seat, the relief so overwhelming it brought tears to her eyes. She didn't bother trying to stem the flow of tears as she imagined how differently things could have ended tonight. She was too exhausted to interrogate him about just who he had watching her grandmother. That was a fight for another day.

Everything was crazy and she had no idea what she was going to do tomorrow, but she was safe right now. That was all she had to hang on to at the moment. And she knew that was all due to Noah.

When Noah finally pulled into the underground parking garage in his building, Lucia was exhausted and wrung out from crying. He pulled around to his usual parking space and turned the car off. His face betrayed no surprise when he looked over and saw her in tears.

"We're going to get this son of a bitch. I promise you that I will not rest until you are safe."

"I know. You've always protected me." She didn't bring up the one day that he hadn't protected her. It was confusing to love and hate him at the same time but it was simply too ingrained in her to think of him as a protector to turn it off now. She just wished she could turn the clock back three weeks to when life had been simple.

She tried to smile but figured by the look on his face that she'd failed miserably. He grimaced and Lucia knew he was thinking of that beautiful and awful night when she'd discovered his secret.

"I know this doesn't mean much to you right now, especially in light of everything that's happened. But I will die before I let anyone ever hurt you."

She knew he meant it. Anyone who wanted to hurt her was going to have to go through Noah first.

Noah helped Lucia down from the Range Rover and his heart melted a little when she clung to him. His heart wasn't the only thing feeling heated. This was the closest she'd let him get to her in weeks.

Shameful

He didn't fool himself that she'd forgiven him. More than likely, she was in shock. He could barely remember the first time he'd truly feared for his life, but the emotions released when fighting were intense and Lucia had been sheltered all her life. She had no idea how to deal with something like this. The horror of having someone try to hurt her. He knew the terror she'd felt at seeing Ryan hurt because he felt the same way.

He kept her close as they walked quickly to get inside the building and onto the elevator. It would be a lot easier to deal with things once he wasn't on edge worried about Lucia's safety. With all the guys there and the amount of security wired into the place, there was literally no safer place for her in the city.

The inside of the loft was already busy. Matthias looked up from his computer when they entered, his eyes immediately going to Lucia. Noah shook his head slightly, hoping that the other man wouldn't say anything about the attack. Lucia looked like she was about to break into a million pieces as it was.

"Let's get you settled," he whispered to her.

Noah held out his arm to indicate that she should precede him. He kept his gaze on the long fall of her hair so his eyes wouldn't be tempted to stray any lower. Lucia was staying with him out of necessity only, not because she'd forgiven him or wanted to be with him. But a guy could hope.

For the first time in his life he really loved someone.

And someone loved him back. Just having even a taste of that, he wasn't ready to let go of it. Deserving or not, he needed her. Needed her love.

Maybe this was his penance for his sins, having the woman he loved right under his nose but still out of reach. She hadn't spoken to him since that tense conversation in the car. He wanted to ask her more about the things she'd been digging into but this wasn't the time. He'd wait until she'd had time to gain her equilibrium back before he asked the hard questions. That was not going to be an easy conversation.

When they reached his room, Lucia shook her head slightly, finally seeming to notice her surroundings.

"Um, Noah? Where am I going to stay?"

He set her bag down on the floor next to his bed. "You can have my room. I don't sleep much anyway, and when I need to crash I'll take one of the spare bedrooms downstairs."

She sat down on the edge of the bed and ran her hands gently over the tangled sheets that he hadn't bothered to straighten that morning. Noah shivered, watching her fingers tracing over the fabric. Why did that affect him as if she'd touched his bare skin?

"I'll get you some clean sheets."

She waved her hand impatiently. "I don't care about that. You know I'm practical, and there's no sense pretending I haven't shared sheets with you before."

He watched as she stood and walked into the en

suite bathroom. When she came out, she'd shed the oversized shirt she'd been wearing and was wearing only a tight camisole and panties.

Noah swallowed hard. Oh Jesus fuck. His dick turned to steel. He fucking missed her. But she didn't need that right now. Right now she needed him to protect her. Right now, he had to earn her trust and her love again. If that was even possible.

She climbed on the bed and pulled the sheets over her, pulling them up until they reached her chin. In that position she looked like a child. *A terrified child.*

"Make yourself comfortable. I have to go brief the team on everything that happened so we can figure out a plan to get this guy." The guy was a fucking ghost and finding him wouldn't be easy, but there was no way he was telling Lucia that.

Lucia nodded. "Okay. I'm just going to read and try to relax a little."

"Good. Text me if you need anything."

She hesitated for a moment. "Uh, Noah?"

"Yeah, Lulu?"

"Thank you. For today. I don't know what I would have done if you weren't there."

He nodded. "You don't have to thank me. Or any of the guys. And nothing's going to happen to you. We're going to see to that."

She burrowed deeper beneath the sheets until only

the top of her head was visible. Noah backed out of the room, pulling the door closed behind him.

Matthias looked up when he came back downstairs. "Is she okay?"

"Not really but she will be. The sooner we figure out who's behind this, the better. Have you heard from Jonas yet?"

Matthias jerked his head in the direction of the conference room. "Yeah, he's here."

"What?"

Noah pushed past him and into the conference room. Jonas stood next to an exhausted and incapacitated Ryan, who was struggling to remain upright while a man wrapped gauze around his arm.

"Seriously, Ry? You should be in the hospital."

Jonas rolled his eyes. "Already told him that. But Superman here thinks that all he needs is a Band-Aid and an aspirin before going back on the job. He woke up before they could get him in the ambulance and refused all further treatment."

Ryan pointed at the man working on his arm. "You joking? This is a flesh wound. You should see the other guy. Besides, I knew that Doctor Breckner does house calls. Tell 'em I'm fine Doc."

Doctor Breckner didn't look amused. "He's *not* fine. He needs stitches and is slightly concussed. And his ribs are bruised. He's lucky he didn't need surgery."

Shameful

Ryan shrugged. "I've had worse. Doesn't sound that bad to me." When he saw their faces, he sighed. "Seriously, I'm fine. Is Lucia okay? I feel like shit Noah. I heard a noise, went in and motherfucker got the jump on me. I fucked that shit right up."

"No, you didn't. You did your job. Anything you remember about him?"

"Tall, like you, and *fast*. Well fucking trained. That was no run of the mill burglar. I cannot wait until we find that asshole. I have all kinds of payback in mind for him."

"You're crazy man. And yes, Lucia is fine. We're all fine. Do you remember anything else that might help us find the son of a bitch?"

Ryan grumbled and cursed. "No. Which fucking pisses me off. Like I said, we fought. I got a few hits in, there was nothing else. Fuck, I'm not even sure how he got in the building. Next thing I know, I'm waking up on a gurney and this fool is telling me I'm on my way to the hospital." Ryan pointed his thumb toward Jonas.

Noah exchanged glances with Jonas. "Ryan is right. The guy was good. Better than good. We fought, no holds barred, and it was like he wasn't even breaking a sweat."

"So I'm right? He's a pro?" Ryan added.

"Yeah, and if he could hold me off with my training and motivation, I guarantee he's been trained by the best. And I promise you, he's not done. He will be back, and we need to fucking be ready because I'm not losing Lucia."

A gasp from the doorway grabbed all of their attention. Noah turned and standing right behind Matthias was … Lucia.

Shit.

"Lucia, are you okay? Do you need anything?" He approached her slowly, happy when she allowed him to pull her into his arms. But when he tried to lead her from the room, she shook off his hold. Damn it. The last thing he had wanted was for her to hear any of that. "Why don't we get you back to the room? You've had a hell of a day. Come on."

But she wasn't having it. "The guy who was in my apartment was a pro? What does that mean? A professional killer?" Her voice rose slightly at the end. "So that hit out on me. It's for real? It isn't some kind of mistake?"

The other guys all glanced at him.

Noah sighed. "We believe that to be the case, yes. But until we catch him, this is all just speculation. But best guess is yes."

She swallowed hard. "Then he isn't going to stop just because he was unsuccessful. He'll be back. And there will be others."

She looked up at Noah and as much as he wanted to, he couldn't lie to her. He never wanted to lie to her again.

"Yes. He'll be back. But this time I'll be ready."

Shameful

Chapter Three

Lucia screamed for her brother. Staring down the man who had shot him, she lifted the gun Rafe had given her and fired. The crack of gunfire startled her awake.

Trying to calm herself, she greedily sucked in deep breaths as she tried to remember all the things the therapist had taught her.

Shameful

Deep breaths. Nice and easy. Do not panic. She was losing it. That nightmare would be the end of her sanity.

Once she steadied her breathing, she reached over to the lamp on her bedside table, trying to turn it on. It was never this dark in her room. Thin slivers of silver moonlight usually peeked through her blinds. She fought the momentary weight of panic and forced her mind to clear. It was only then that she remembered she wasn't at home.

She shuddered at the thought of the man in her apartment. He was intent on killing her, intent on killing Noah. He'd already given Ryan a concussion. God only knew what he would have done to her.

What if he'd hurt Noah? What if he'd *killed* Noah? Would she have minded?

The answer surprised her, because she *would*. Not just because she wanted the pleasure of doing it herself, but also because she cared about him. That reason was more frustrating than anything else. After everything he'd put her through, everything he had done. She worried about him. Because she cared. It was impossible to stop loving him even though she knew what he was.

You are a damn glutton for punishment.

She wished she could set fire to her feelings and watch them burn in a pyre down to ashes with no regrets. But she couldn't. Despite his lies, he'd taken care of her, even when she didn't want him to. He took care of Nonna and looked out for her.

He was *still* looking out for her.

With a growl, she yanked back her covers. She fumbled around for her phone, finally finding it on the opposite nightstand and checking the time. Damn. Only a little after 4 in the morning. *Far too early to get up.*

After that nightmare, she was neither tired nor was she in a hurry to return to the clutches of the shadow dreams. With bare feet she padded over to the door, slowly creeping it open. Surprisingly it was dark, save for the iridescent nightlights lining the walls.

Okay, just a drink of water then back to bed.

Somehow, a part of her had always imagined that Noah's office was always open. That somehow he and the men who worked for him were superheroes like the Justice League or something. But apparently even superheroes needed sleep. Besides, she knew better. These guys were no heroes.

Well, maybe the others were, but *Noah* certainly wasn't.

When she reached the kitchen, she dragged a glass out of the cabinet. Suddenly, all of the lights flickered on and she squeaked and jumped, whipping around.

"Oh shit. Sorry. I didn't realize anyone was in here. I just came for—"

Lucia put up a hand. "No, it's fine. I was the one skulking around in the dark."

Matthias nodded. His eyes went wide, and he somehow managed to look every which way but directly at her. Oh no. He was pissed. She'd had him lie to Noah. And now Noah was undoubtedly pissed. That was her fault.

"Matthias, listen—"

He started talking at the same time that she did. "Lucia, look I never meant to—"

And then he gestured to her. "Ladies first," he said with a smile. He still wouldn't look directly at her, nor did he come any further into the kitchen. Instead, he hung by the wall. But he'd certainly come in here for a reason.

"Look, Matthias. I'm so sorry. I never should have dragged you into this and had you looking for information for me. I certainly never should've asked you to keep it from Noah, your boss. I know how he is and I know you were trying to help me, but I was wrong to ask you to do that."

His eyes flickered to her and quickly looked away again. "Lucia, it's fine. It was my choice to comply or not. I chose not to tell him, but I'm sorry I broke your confidence and told him anyway. I was worried you were in danger and, as it turns out, you *were*. If it had been simple information, I never would've told him."

She rounded the giant island in the kitchen and approached him. He immediately took a step back. Looking even further away from her if that was possible.

Damn, he was so mad at her. "Matthias, I consider you a friend. And I used that. And that makes me a bad person and I'm really sorry. I hope that you can find a way to forgive me."

He frowned but still didn't look at her. "Forgive you? Honestly, it's fine. I would do anything to help you. You're family. I'm not mad."

Lucia stared up at him. Then she planted her hands on her hips. "Oh yeah, then why is it that you can't look at me?" She opened her arms. "Can we hug this out, start fresh? I won't take advantage of our friendship again. I promise."

Matthias flushed and hugged the wall like she had cooties. Like the last thing on earth he wanted to do was hug her. Maybe he *wasn't* a hugger? No, they had hugged dozens of times.

Fine.

If Matthias wouldn't come to the mountain then she would bring the mountain to Matthias. She closed the distance between them, her bare feet barely making a sound on the concrete. And then she wrapped her arms around him tight. *Go ahead and escape this hug*, she thought. But Matthias didn't escape. It took a second, but then he wrapped his arms around her. She had never noticed how tall he was, and he was nearly as solid as Noah.

Geez, did Matthias have muscle? Why hadn't she ever paid attention before?

She'd always taken the mildly geeky exterior, with the glasses and superhero T-shirts, and categorized him as a nerd. Which to her usually meant soft. How had she never noticed that her friend had muscles?

Granted, they weren't like Noah's. No one had

muscles like Noah. She knew she was probably biased, but still.

"I'm really sorry, Matthias."

"You have nothing to be sorry about."

She didn't know how long they stood there, but then Noah's voice came from behind, cold and furious. "What the fuck do you think you're doing running around here naked?"

Matthias immediately released her, but Lucia took longer to step back. When she turned to face Noah, she took in the sight of his boxers and his completely bare chest, and damn it, she salivated. That didn't mean she didn't still hate him. It didn't mean she wasn't still furious with him, and it didn't mean that she trusted him. All it meant was that she was human. The man looked good.

Good enough to lick, honestly. And she had.

There was still so much she wanted to try with him, so much they hadn't had a chance to do. All the things she'd heard JJ talk about, she wanted to try with Noah. *Well, now you're not going to because, hello, we hate him.*

Yes, she hated him. But that didn't mean she didn't want to lick him. And somehow, simultaneously, she wanted to murder him, too.

"I am not naked." She slid a glance down at herself, slightly flushing. Shit. She hadn't put on shorts. She slid a glance to Matthias, who was looking anywhere but at her *or* Noah. "Sorry. I'm not used to having to cover up." She turned to Noah. "Besides, you're the one who told me to make myself at home."

Through gritted teeth, he ground out, "That doesn't mean run around here naked. Matthias is here. Or did you forget?"

"I was just coming for some water. No one was supposed to be awake. The lights were freaking off. Bite me."

From behind her, Matthias scoffed. Noah's eyes glinted and his smile went menacing and predatory. "Anytime. You just tell me where."

And then something happened to her body. It was like her lady parts had softened, readying her body for him to have her against any flat surface. Hell, screw a flat surface. The wall would do if necessary.

Why did he do that to her? She didn't like him. *You don't have to like him to want him.* Wasn't that the truth? But the last thing on earth she was ever going to do was let him know that.

"Sorry, Noah. Not interested. What's that thing that guys say sometimes? I'm just not that into you?"

And with that, she turned and headed back for her bedroom. She could feel Noah's eyes on her ass. Let him look all he wanted, because he was never going to touch it again.

Shameful

Did she just—she just walked away from—*what* the hell? Noah glared at Matthias. She'd had her hands all over the kid. Noah had to work hard at not killing him right now out of pure jealousy. "Keep it shut."

Matthias put up his hands, but the kid's lips twitched as if he was fighting back a laugh. "You got it boss. Keeping it shut."

But Noah wasn't in the mood. He never slept anyway, but the moment he'd heard Lucia's voice he'd snapped awake and he'd gone looking for her. The image of her wrapped around another man was enough to make his trigger finger itch.

He didn't want her wrapped around Matthias. What he wanted was the two of them in his bed, her underneath him, over him, in front of him.

Never going to happen again. Stop living in your fairy tale. Deal with the problem at hand.

But since he'd lived that fairy tale, it was impossible to let it go. Especially as his dick kept coming up with elaborate schemes to get her back in bed. Most of which sounded totally doable in the moment.

"You want to tell me what you were doing with your hands on her considering she's not wearing any clothes?"

Matthias swallowed hard but shook his head. "Noah, I didn't touch her. She came over here and hugged *me*. I think she could tell I was deliberately not looking at her."

"Damn straight you weren't looking at her. Not if you want to keep your goddamned eyeballs."

There was that lip twitch thing from the kid again. "I like my eyeballs where they are, thanks."

"You seemed to be hugging her back." Noah narrowed his gaze.

Matthias rolled his eyes. "Mate, Lucia is family. Of course I hugged her back. I'm not mad at her, and *I'm* not the one she's mad at. If she's handing out free hugs, I'm taking them. If you want some hugs of your own, you might want to talk to her."

Noah stared at Matthias. He wasn't usually so defiant. He knew the kid looked up to him. Granted he could use some better idols. He also knew the kid knew enough to fear him a little. "Yeah, you might be right about that." Except so far no amount of talking or apologizing was working. But as he watched her ass stroll down the hall, he knew he had to keep trying.

Noah followed after Lucia, knowing it was probably a bad idea. But lately he was full of all kinds of bad ideas. He grabbed the door before she could slam it behind her. "Lucia, wait."

She pushed against the door. "Noah, what am I

waiting for? We don't have anything to say to each other. You were right. Someone is trying to kill me. They broke into my apartment, and one of your men is injured because of me. So I'll listen to you. I'll do what you want, shut up, and go where I'm told. The only thing I ask is to be able to work. And for you to not talk to me, touch me, or even look at me."

"Sorry, I can't do that last part."

She opened the door and Noah nearly tumbled in. "Why? Why can't you? Because you had no problem lying to me for years, watching me struggle and suffer. Now, when I ask you to do something that would actually help me recover from that, you refuse to do it?"

"You don't understand." Noah lowered his voice so only she could hear him. "Ever since I touched you, I can't help but think about it. So if it's more convenient for you, if it makes things easier for you, I will try. But I have to look out for you. I just can't help it."

"You're telling me you can't help it? Try, or better yet, *talk* to me. Tell me what the hell is going on. Tell me who that man in my apartment was, or at least who you think he was. Something tells me you weren't surprised to see him there. Something tells me you *expected* him to be there. And you keep saying my life is in danger. I think you know who's after me."

Noah sighed. He couldn't tell her. She knew that he was the one who'd hurt Rafe, but she didn't know the rest. The rest would shatter any possibility she ever had of trusting him again. He knew how she felt about him. Hate was a strong word, but right now she was so far past hate. She wanted to completely annihilate him for life. Not that he blamed her.

"You know I can't tell you that."

She crossed her arms and stared him down. "So far, my experience is when you say things like *can't*, you mean *won't*. I don't want to hear about how it's for my own good or how you're protecting me. I'm done unless you are going to start talking to me, treating me like I'm someone who deserves to know the truth. Otherwise, I have no interest in saying anything to you."

"Lucia, this is in your best interest."

"You keep saying that. You've broken into my place, you've chased off boyfriends that might've liked me. You've interfered in my life by paying for my apartment and paying for Nonna's house. You have interjected yourself in every aspect of my life, so much so that I'm not even allowed to live it for myself. Then I find out you killed my brother. I ask you for answers, anything, and you think that taciturn bullshit is going to work on me?" She sneered at him. "Get the hell out of my room. I don't want to see you. I don't want to talk to you. I'm done. As a matter of fact, you might want to transfer my case to some other security firm or something, because I don't want to be anywhere near you."

"It's nice to want things, princess. Trust me, I wish you didn't have to know. I wish we could just go back to being Noah and Lucia, and I could tease you and you not be mad at me anymore. But we can't. This is real life now, real brass tacks. I'll do my job and stay out of your way, but I'm not going to hurt you anymore than I have to."

Noah turned and walked out, very gently closing the door behind him. The anger simmered just under his skin. He hated the way she looked at him now. Contempt, distrust— it was all there. She was right. He had interjected himself into her life. At the time, he had told himself he was protecting her, keeping an eye on things, making sure she didn't need anything.

She was right. It was selfish.

He was just trying to assuage his guilt over Rafe. And now, he'd hurt the only person in his life he'd ever cared about. The only person he was even capable of loving. Actually, make that the two people. *Rafe and Lucia.*

He stormed back toward his room, catching Matthias in the kitchen as he scarfed down the remnants of a key lime pie. "You're on Lucia duty tomorrow. She's got some fitting for the show, I think."

Matthias stopped, fork midway to mouth. "Okay, who am I going with?"

Noah sighed. "We're stretched thin. I think I can send Dylan. We'll put him in the audience while you're back stage with Lucia. There's a lot of security already there. The event has security to protect the models, so we'll use the set up to help protect her."

Matthias nodded. "We'll make it happen."

Noah rolled the tension out of his shoulders. He hadn't been able to sleep because he kept picturing how she would look at him all day tomorrow. Plus, he was needed on another job. He hated not being there to protect her, but he would make sure there was someone there who could. She trusted Matthias, as evidenced by the way she'd wrapped her little body around him. Noah suppressed the twinge of jealousy. Matthias was a kid. He'd worked hard to save the kid's life so killing him now would be counterproductive.

"Good. Call me if there are any issues."

"Will do, boss."

Noah stomped back to bed, as if he were going to get any sleep anyway. He might as well just get in a workout, because every time he was around Lucia, his thoughts kept him up.

Because you want more. More of what happened that night three weeks ago when he had altered her world. Well, just like he'd told Lucia, it *was* nice to want things. Unfortunately in this case, he was never going to get what he wanted again.

Chapter Four

"Okay, Hettie, put this on. No, we don't have time to alter it. Just suck in and make it work."

Lucia grabbed her head between her hands and squeezed. They had less than thirty minutes until show time and somehow she'd managed to lose a belt that had been right in her hand, one of the girls had accidentally spilled a drink on herself and was all sticky, and another somehow didn't fit into a garment that she'd fit perfectly just the prior week. It was as if the fashion show gods were displeased with her and decided to make everything go wrong simultaneously. With everything else going on in her life lately, she didn't need this.

Please just let me pull this off, she thought.

Matthias appeared at the door to the dressing area. When he took in her expression and the sheepish model standing behind her, he raised his eyebrows slightly. "Everything okay?"

"Yes, I just need about five extra pairs of arms. That's all."

Once Noah had understood how important this show was, he'd stopped trying to convince her to stay home, so that was a win. However, he'd insisted on her keeping Matthias with her backstage while Dylan was in the audience. She'd been trying to think of good excuses to explain his presence, but so far everyone had just accepted that he was a friend. The fact that he was cute went a long way toward their acceptance.

The model behind her eyed Matthias with interest. She snorted. They were probably all assuming she'd brought her boyfriend along. The fact that this hadn't stopped anyone from flirting with him was pretty sad in her opinion. It was a good thing he wasn't actually her boyfriend or she would have been annoyed.

"Hettie, my friend Matthias is helping me out today. I hope you don't mind."

Hettie tossed her mile long blond hair extensions over her shoulder. "I don't mind at all. He's a cutie. Why are all the cutest guys batting for the other team? So unfair."

Lucia froze.

Matthias blinked. The smile on his face faded slightly. "Batting for the other team? No, I'm on our—."

"Yeah, we don't mind," Annie chirped before he could finish. "He's *soooo* cute."

"Really cute." Another one of the models stroked a hand gently over his hair.

Matthias turned red and mumbled something about making a phone call. Lucia couldn't help laughing. They were going to give the poor guy a heart attack.

While she was inspecting Annie to make sure she'd cleaned all the spilled soda off her skin, Adriana walked by and quirked an eyebrow.

"Let's go!"

Lucia jumped up and grabbed her phone. The models all fell in line and stood still while Adriana inspected them. For the next hour, Lucia tried her best to keep up and stay out of the way when appropriate. But this was probably the only thing that could take her mind off the events of the past twenty-four hours. She'd been dreaming about being backstage at a major fashion show since she was a teenager and now she was here. She peeked around the curtain and watched as the next to last model strutted down the runway. As many times as she'd watched fashion shows online, nothing captured the pure electricity like being there. A million camera flashes lit up the space like a fireworks display.

Then there was a sudden hum, and the entire room was plunged into darkness. The cameras kept flashing, which made the sudden darkness even more jarring. At first the crowd was quiet, and then the murmur of voices got louder as people started to panic. Someone screamed.

Lucia went still as her brain tried to make sense of what was happening. There was a brush of movement behind her, and a shiver stole down her back. *Stop, that's Matthias.*

But then someone moved again and wrapped an arm around her waist, their other hand snaking around her face. Every cell in her body said run, scream, fight. She opened her mouth to scream but opted to bite down instead. Whoever it was grunted, and she took three steps forward.

Then someone grabbed her arm. And this time she screamed.

"It's okay, it's just me."

Lucia sagged with relief at the sound of Matthias' voice. "Oh, God, I thought—" She couldn't finish the thought. Had she imagined that hand snaking around her? "What's going on?"

"I don't know, but we need to get the hell out of

here. Follow me."

When he grabbed her hand, she allowed him to lead her. Her sense of direction was usually pretty good, but before long she had no idea where they were in the building. It felt like an endless stream of twists and turns. Finally, there was a soft, slow whine. The sound of a door closing.

Something was wrong. Matthias, who would normally have put her at ease, wasn't saying anything. Lucia was scared to say anything since she wasn't sure who was near them and might overhear, so she bit her lip and counted down from one hundred in her head. After a few minutes, Matthias pulled out his phone and started typing a text.

"Dylan didn't see anything before the power outage, so maybe this has nothing to do with us." He didn't sound convinced, though, and Lucia wasn't either.

Seriously, what were the odds of there being a power outage randomly the day after someone broke into her apartment? She shivered. This was the perfect opportunity for someone to grab her. If Matthias hadn't gotten to her first, someone could have knocked her out the same way they'd gotten to Ryan.

"How are we going to get out of here?" she whispered.

"We aren't. If someone is looking for you, I'm not going to put you in their path. We'll be safe here while Dylan investigates. I scouted this closet as a possible safe spot when I did my rounds earlier."

There was another sudden hum, and the lights came on. Lucia blinked in the bright lights as her eyes adjusted. She gasped when she saw Matthias crouched next to her with an intense look on his face and a surprisingly large gun in his hand.

"Where did that come from?"

Matthias gave her a strange look. "My holster. Did you think I was protecting you with a water gun or something?"

She laughed nervously. He was right; it was a stupid question. But she didn't know how to say that she'd been unprepared to see him looking like a real bodyguard because that wasn't how she saw him. He'd already had to deal with models assuming he was gay and treating him like a cute mascot today. Although if those girls had seen him like this, all fierce and determined, they might not have been so quick to treat him like a little boy.

"Of course not. I just couldn't tell where you'd hidden it before. That's a … really big gun."

Luckily Matthias didn't pause to analyze her silly statement. He pulled her to her feet gently. "Once Dylan gives us the okay, we'll go back to grab your things and then get out of here. No need to stick around, right?"

"Yeah, the show was basically over." She'd get shit for leaving early but she was hoping that all the confusion would cover her early departure.

Seeing Matthias in full bodyguard mode had

snapped her out of the confused state she'd been in since yesterday. This was serious and it was happening, and she wasn't just going to sit back and do nothing.

If some asshole was going to come for her, she wasn't going to just let him.

Noah was running on the treadmill when he saw Matthias's name show up on his phone. He'd been out on a job that morning and had only gotten back a short while ago. That Lucia was exposed at that damn fashion show had been in the back of his mind the whole time. He'd agreed not to interfere in her life more than necessary,

but it didn't mean he had to like it.

Since he knew Matthias was with Lucia, he hit the emergency stop button and grabbed the phone.

"What's going on? Is Lucia okay?"

"Everything is fine. But there was an incident at the show. A power outage."

As Noah listened, his heart rate slowly went back to normal. He clapped a hand over his chest. If he reacted this way to just the idea of Lucia being hurt, he didn't want to think about the future if he failed to keep her safe. Hell no. Not a possibility.

"We're almost at the loft now. Just wanted to let you know what was going on. Dylan stayed behind to talk to some of the people in the audience."

"Great. Just get in here."

Noah hung up and then took a quick shower. Then he walked back to the main area of the loft to fill in Jonas. This was the second incident they'd had while protecting Lucia. Everyone on the team needed to be briefed because her situation was now considered high risk. If it had been a random break in at her place, the likelihood that she'd be attacked again would be very low. But clearly, nothing about this was random. Someone was determined to get to her and they'd just proven that they weren't going to give up until they got what they wanted.

Noah clenched his fists at the thought. What they wanted was Lucia. So whoever these assholes were that were targeting her, they'd just become number one on his shit list. He didn't care how many resources he had to dedicate, they weren't getting anywhere near Lucia.

Noah and Jonas were still standing there talking when Matthias and a very shaken Lucia walked in. Noah's first instinct was to grab her and hold her. He'd already taken a few steps in her direction before it all came back to him. They weren't together anymore.

She hates you now, remember? You're the source of all her nightmares. The last thing she's going to want is comfort from you.

Before he could say anything, Matthias started

talking. "It appears to have been a false alarm. But the show was basically over anyway, so I figured it was better to get the hell out of there."

Noah took his eyes away from Lucia long enough to clap a hand on Matthias's back. The kid had done well even though this wasn't his usual thing.

"You made the right call. After you fill the others in, why don't you check with the power company and find out which areas were affected by the outage. That might help us pinpoint whether it was truly random or part of a targeted attack."

Matthias nodded, and Noah could tell he was happy to have something tangible to do.

He turned to Lucia. "Don't worry. We're going to figure out who is behind this. They won't touch you. I promise."

She nodded but looked like she was on the verge of crying. Noah cursed himself internally. He wanted nothing more than to be able to pull her into his arms and wipe away those tears but that wasn't what she wanted from him anymore. He'd lied to her too many times. Even though it was for her own good, there was just too much deceit between them now for her to ever trust him again. Even knowing how things would end between them, Noah wouldn't go back and change things. He'd done what he had to do in order to protect her and even if that meant they couldn't be together, he'd take her safety over his own happiness any day.

After standing there awkwardly for a few seconds, Lucia surprised them both when she pushed past Noah to envelope Matthias in a hug. "Thanks for coming with me today, Matthias. I really appreciate it."

Matthias wore an expression that was a cross between elation at the hug and fear at what Noah's response would be. He kept glancing over as if expecting Noah to pull out a weapon and ice him right then and there.

Noah gritted his teeth. He wasn't that bad, was he? Okay, maybe he was, but not in this case. He was happy that Lucia trusted the others enough to follow their directions in the heat of a situation.

Matthias walked in the direction of his room, and Noah followed Lucia. She dropped her handbag on the floor next to the bed before slipping out of her shoes. After glancing at him worriedly, she took her jeans off, too. Noah had never been jealous of an inanimate object before, but in that moment, watching as she slipped beneath the sheets with a sigh, he would have gladly traded places with his bed. Lucia let out a long sigh that told him better than any words could have just how scary and exhausting the day had been.

"Matthias was amazing back there," she murmured. "He grabbed me and led me to a closet to hide. When the lights came on and I saw him holding that huge gun, I don't know, it brought it all home for me. This isn't just about me. If we don't figure this thing out then so many people could potentially be hurt and that's not what I want."

"That's not what I want either. I swear we're doing

everything we can to figure this out."

She rolled over until she was facing him directly. "But we haven't done the most obvious thing. This entire time we've been tiptoeing around each other, but we can't ignore the elephant in the room forever. This whole thing started because I was asking the wrong questions. Or I guess they were the right questions."

Noah ran his hands over his head. It shouldn't be this hard to talk about everything, considering what she'd already discovered. But if they were going to get to the bottom of this, Lucia was right. They needed to get it all out in the open. Which meant telling her things he'd always hoped he could take to his grave.

"You're right."

"I am?" Lucia sat up, looking shocked.

Noah would have laughed at her astonishment but truly it was a sad commentary on how often he'd kept her on the outside of his life. There was very little that she knew of his life before he'd met Rafe. He still wasn't ready to spill that whole story and honestly, it wasn't relevant. What they needed to talk about was *that day*. That horrible day when he'd made a mistake and her brother had paid the price.

"It's time we had a talk."

Chapter Five

"Before we do that, I have to ask. You're sure you're okay?" Noah's voice was soft.

She shook her head. Her body was still tense, arms wrapped around herself as if they were the only things holding her together. "The lights went dark. Someone tried to put a hand over my mouth. And the next thing I knew,

Shameful

Matthias had me in a closet. It was pandemonium and we couldn't get out, so he locked us in a closet with his gun trained on the door."

Noah cursed low under his breath. "The kid did good."

She glared up at him. "He's no kid, Noah. I mean, you should have seen the look in his eyes. He was ready to kill whoever tried to hurt me. I've never seen him like that. Who is he? That guy out there," she pointed in the direction of the door. "He's no kid. He is not at all the guy I thought he was. What happened to sweet, affable Matthias? Computer nerd. You know the guy who can't say no to me? At the show, he was lethal. Deadly. I didn't even recognize him."

Noah sighed and spoke quietly. "That's kind of the point of having a bodyguard. It's better when they seem unassuming. But don't mistake Matthias for your favorite plush toy. The kid is dangerous." He slid his glance away from her. "We all are."

Matthias more than some, Noah thought. He would have to talk to him.

He worked hard to keep Matthias away from violence usually. The kid went to the dark and scary places too easily. He always worried he'd pulled Matthias out too late. That ORUS had already broken him. Tainted him. Turned him into the kind of killer that didn't even think. But they'd have that conversation another time. Right now, Matthias had done his job. He'd protected Lucia. Put himself between her and a bullet … or worse. That was all that mattered. Or at least that was all that mattered to Noah. Lucia, on the other hand, was furious.

"Noah, you didn't see what I saw. I swear to God, he would've shot me somewhere nonlethal if he thought that would shut me up and get me to comply. I've never seen him like that before."

Noah knew she had to come around on her own. She and Matthias would have to talk about it. "He did his job. And right now, all I am is grateful."

A shudder tore through her body, and all Noah wanted to do was pull her close, take her against him, tell her everything would be all right. But that was a lie. Because nothing was all right, and it wasn't going to be until he found a way to stop this hit.

"Noah, I just want some answers. And then I want to sleep. Sleep for a very long time."

He didn't know when he decided to do it. Tell her the truth. All he knew was in that moment she held herself together by sheer will and arms that were too thin. So he told her everything.

"Lucia, I know how much you loved Rafe. And I wish to God every day that he was here. But there was a side to Rafe you didn't know. He's the one who trained me. The one who was my mentor. He taught me everything I know. How to be the *best* assassin. How to be the *quietest* assassin. He taught me how to talk my way into and out of places. He taught me how to sneak in silently and never leave a trace of myself behind."

When he finally glanced over at her face, she stared at him, mouth agape.

"So what are you saying? That *Rafe* was some kind of killer?"

Noah paused. He wanted to be honest with her. Tell her as much as he could, but he had to find a way to keep her safe. To not compromise her.

"Yes. I will tell you as much as I can. I won't tell you the organization we worked for. I'm probably telling you way too much as it is. Do you understand the stakes now? This isn't a matter of me playing games with you, or keeping you in the dark. It's a matter of me trying my damnedest to keep you alive. I'm doing anything it takes to manage that."

She stared at him. "Rafe killed people?"

Noah swallowed hard. Then gave her a brusque nod. "And so do I. At least I used to. I left the organization shortly after Rafe's death. We were supposed to be doing things for a good cause. Taking out the worst of the worst. But after my friend, my mentor, was gone, I just couldn't anymore. As part of my negotiation for release in my contract, I took Matthias with me. In so many ways, the kid is just like me. Too good at killing. Too good at being dark."

Lucia shook her head. "I don't understand any of this."

He shoved his hands in his pockets and started

pacing. He couldn't stand still and wait, watching for the hatred and derision to cross her face. So he walked the length of the room.

"When I was sixteen, I was mostly on my own. Technically I was still considered a ward of the state. They had me listed as being in a foster home but about that point, I discovered that the foster homes were more likely to kill me than being on the street. So as often as I could, I made my escape."

She frowned. "Where were the people that were supposed to protect you?"

He shrugged. "Unfortunately in the foster care system, those people are few and far between. And they're so overwhelmed with their caseloads, paying attention when one sixteen-year-old spends more time on the streets than he does with the family that's supposed to be feeding him is hard." He shook his head. "Anyway, I was what you would call a petty thief. I was real good with sleight-of-hand. Real good with distractions. And women. I was a terror. I recognized young that women got a little hung up on my face. It made them easy marks. All I had to do was dress nice. Show the lady a little attention and then I'd have the contents of her purse in no time. Sleight-of-hand here, a little misdirection there, and I was usually in and out without anyone being the wiser. I stayed away from things like burglary and other things that could go wrong, but I was still nothing but a common thief."

Noah kept walking; he didn't dare stop to watch her

face. He didn't dare stop to see what she thought of him now. He just kept moving.

"One night I was supposed to be doing a job with some friends in the theater district, but they hadn't showed. They probably got a bigger score and didn't want to cut me in. So I crossed a couple of avenues, was going to do the job on my own, but in the back of this alleyway next to this Chinese restaurant, I heard a groan. It sounded like someone was in a world of hurt. Normally you learn quick and early to avoid those kinds of sounds, and honestly, I don't know what made me stop that night. But I did. And I found Ian."

Lucia frowned. "Who's Ian?"

"He's the one who told me you're in danger. He's also the man responsible for turning me into a killer. Sure, it wasn't by his hand directly. But saving him that night put me on a particular path. One I didn't quite know how to get off of. One I didn't *want* to get off of."

"He was an assassin, too?"

Noah nodded. "He got hurt on the job. I won't bore you with the details but I dragged him to a safe place to lie low. My friends and I would use it to stash the stolen goods we usually grabbed. It was an abandoned studio no one ever went to. The building was pretty much condemned. I don't even know how I managed it because he was in a bad way.

"But I managed to half-carry, half-drag him over there. I kept an eye on him. He had some nasty knife wounds. But he walked me through the whole first-aid thing. It was my first battle triage." He shrugged. "It wouldn't be my last. Anyway, I brought him food and water for the next couple of days after. Once he was on the mend, he asked for my help to get him to a safe house. From there, my life completely changed. Rafe was assigned as my partner. Assigned to teach me, to look out for me. Honestly, I don't think your brother was too enthusiastic about that at first. But then he sort of took to it. I guess he already had practice being a big brother to you."

She shook her head. "I still can't get over the fact that you're telling me that you and my brother were assassins."

"I don't want to tell you any of this. I know how you already look at me. I know how you'll look at me when I finish telling you everything. I'm doing that with eyes wide open because right now, if I don't tell you, you won't be able to protect yourself if you need to."

She stared at him. "So what happened to Rafe? I know that you were the one who shot him. But why? If he was like your brother, why would you kill him? Why do that to me? To Nonna?"

Noah stopped directly in front of her. He sat on the edge of the bed so he could meet her gaze. "That day I had a target. And so you know, I won't be using names right now. I'm trying to keep you as shielded from this I can. The target was a major player in a drug cartel. Until then, no one had been able to get close enough to take either him or his boss out. The word was that the head of the cartel was no longer the man in charge, but rather a puppet. Word was that our target was the real man in charge.

"The way my former employers used to work, when a government organization couldn't do the legal thing, they'd call us to do the shadow thing. All I knew was that I had my orders. For years, everyone had been trying to get in with the cartel leader. And I finally found an easy way in. His daughter. That part was easier than I thought. She was young. About my age when I started. Seventeen, barely. I managed to talk my way into her school when they were having a sports day. Hundreds of students from other schools were there. It was easy to get past the security. I chatted her up, and the next thing she knew, we were dating. Just a few weeks, all very innocent. But she wanted me to meet her father, and that was my in. It was a risk, sending me in with a gun. So, we managed it with a 3-D one. For several days, I sent her presents with parts of the gun hidden in the boxes and the wrappings. When I finally went to her house, I asked her to bring me everything I had sent her, including the specially made bullets. None of it was metal, so even if the security guards used the wand metal detector on me, they wouldn't have found it. It was brilliant."

The horror froze on Lucia's face. "But Noah, you could've been killed."

"I am very well aware of that. In truth, I had no business being there. I'd done more than a few jobs with

Rafe. That's how we worked, two-man teams. When one fell, there was a backup built-in."

He tried not to take her shuddering too personally. It was a wonder she wasn't running away from him with her hair on fire.

"I begged the higher-ups in the organization for solo jobs. I wanted to prove myself. Everyone kept talking about how much of a natural I was. How good I was at all of it. You needed someone to run a deception plan; I was your guy. You wanted someone to run surveillance; I was good at not being seen. You name it, I could be that guy. And I wanted to prove myself. In our organization, failure was not tolerated. I wanted to show my worth outside of Rafe. So I volunteered. In truth it was too big a job for just one of us. It should have been a two-man job. I was no doubt going to get myself killed. But I didn't see it that way. Get in, take out the target, and get out. All I had to do was finish the job." Noah hung his head in shame. "I was cocky. That's what got your brother killed."

"Why did you shoot him?" Her voice quivered.

Before Noah knew what was happening, the sorrow and grief he'd been holding back all this time bubbled to the surface. His eyes stung and he worked to hold back the tears. But they wouldn't be dammed. He had to get it all out. He had to tell her the truth.

"I honestly don't know what happened. It was simple. The plan was go in with the girl, which I managed. Meet her father. Stick around. It was his birthday celebration. Take out the target, egress through to the south side where there was a boat waiting. Simple. But that's not how it worked out."

"What went wrong?"

"Sure, I made it in the house. Sure, I met her father. While everyone was drinking and laughing at his 70th birthday party, I had my target in sight. He'd slipped away from the party. I followed him. I'd already taken care of the cameras, so no one would see me in the security feed. What I didn't count on was Rafe. I didn't count on him coming into the courtyard and stepping in front of my bullet. He didn't want me to do it. I can still hear him screaming, 'No. Noah don't.'"

He shook his head. "I hear that over and over and over again. I never understood why. But I was in such a hurry to prove myself. No, in a hurry to prove that I could do the job. That I deserved every chance to come my way. I had a target. Our targets were the scum of the earth. I was doing my job. I was being the good soldier." He sighed. "Or so I thought. I never expected Rafe to jump in front of that gun. I never expected that bullet to hit him. It's a nightmare I live with every single day. Seeing my best friend go down. Seeing the man who trained me, the man who loved me like a brother or father would. Knowing I was the one responsible."

Lucia sat forward. "What happened from there? All I know is that I shot you. I don't remember anything else."

"After I shot Rafe, my target was on the run. He

immediately started to bolt, and I should've gone after him but I couldn't. I couldn't leave my best friend lying there. Before I could even move there was the crack of another gunshot, but this one came from the wrong direction. A direction I didn't expect. That one came from you."

"I'd followed him. I heard the gunshots," she whispered.

"With the pain of the bullet, I knew that I absolutely deserved what was happening. But then in my peripheral vision, I saw that it was you. I knew there was no way Rafe would've wanted you to see what you'd seen. He wouldn't have wanted you anywhere near that mess. By that time, the gunshots had alerted the guards and they were coming toward us. I couldn't let them find you." He glanced at her and then dropped his head into his hands. "I saw you collapse. I knew your brother was gone, so I went directly for you. I had to keep you safe. It's what he would have wanted. He wouldn't want those monsters with their hands on you."

Lucia shuddered again, her eyes going vacant while her mind tried to put the pieces together. "Oh my God. You made sure I got home?"

He nodded solemnly. "I failed my mission. And Rafe was down. I'd hit him dead center mass with three bullets. I'd fucked up. But I could get to you. So I made the choice; I chose you instead of Rafe. I took you to the south side, to my exit. I knew my people would be looking for me. Wanting to know what happened, switching the boat to the opposite side of the island. You were so out of it. Complete and total shock. I wasn't sure if you knew what was happening. You were practically catatonic at that point. I didn't know what else to do, so I took you to the safest place I could think of. The ice cream place at the Wingate Hotel. That was where one of the island's only payphones was. I called the police, and I called the Feds for you. As soon as you were safe I went back for him. But the place was already crawling with cops. From that point on, all I could do was follow the usual protocol— get back on my egress route, and have my people get me out of there. But I made sure you were safe first."

Lucia dragged in shallow breaths. "I couldn't remember any of it. I blocked it all out. For years, I asked you what happened."

He swiped at his eyes. "I'm so sorry I had to lie to you. I was terrified you'd wake up one day and remember everything. Remember that I was there. That I was the one who shot Rafe. That I was the one who took you away. But you didn't. Even after your time with the therapist. I tried to stay away from you, I did. I swear to God. I tried to just look out for you the best that I could but every time I turned around, you were there, insisting I speak to you. You were calling me, asking for advice, telling me when Nonna needed something, and inviting me to dinner. And the guilt turned. I could do for you what I had failed to do for Rafe. I could protect you. I could step in as big brother. I could keep you from harm. It was the least I could do for him."

"All that time? Why did you even save me?"

"Isn't that obvious by now? I have loved you since long before I knew that it was hazardous to my health. Deviating from the plan was necessary to keep you out of the crosshairs of the people that I worked for. At the time, no one seemed to notice the delay from me making my egress route to calling back to home base. The only person who noticed was Matthias. He didn't say a word. He protected you, too. It was one of the reasons I pulled him out of there. I knew he could be trusted."

Noah watched her closely, worried. She looked a little green around the gills, like she might throw up.

"Lucia, that's everything. I'm not lying to you. I know you don't believe me, and I have no right to ask for your forgiveness. I tore this rift between us, and I have no idea how to rectify it. Not that I can. All I can do is what Rafe would want. Which is to keep you out of harm's way."

"Were you ever going to tell me any of this?"

She spoke so softly he wasn't sure he'd heard her correctly.

"I wish I didn't have to tell you now. The people I used to work for, they're ruthless. I don't want you anywhere near that part of my life. But things are out of my hands now. That guy they sent to your apartment, they aren't fucking around. I've managed to avoid a war with them for a long time. But that truce was broken the moment they started coming after you. If they want war, I'll take one to them."

Shameful

"Why did you start staying with me? Wouldn't it have been better for you to stay away?" She didn't sound upset about it, merely perplexed.

He cleared his throat. "It would have been so much safer to stay in the periphery of your life. But I couldn't. Because I cared too much. That was my mistake. And now it will probably cost you your life."

"You, Noah Blake, you could have had any woman. Why me? Was that part of the plan? To keep me from remembering? To keep me so distracted with your general assholery and eventually so weak with good sex that my brain never worked?"

His head snapped up. "I wanted you long before I even knew what to do with you. What's been happening over the last couple of months—I haven't been able to fight that any more than I could *not* protect you. To me, this is real. But I never wanted *this*, who I am, to touch you. This was never supposed to be part of your world. I know I'm not good enough for you. And now you know it too."

They sat like that for a long moment— Noah with his hands covering his face. Lucia watching him. When she finally spoke again, her voice was mellow.

"I always felt there was something with us. Even when I couldn't recognize it. Back then, after he died? I knew there was something about the way you protected me. And that nothing bad was ever going to happen when you were looking out for me."

"You should feel that way. Because it's true."

She licked her lips nervously. "I don't know what to do with my feelings about you and my brother. Knowing what you've just told me, I have so many more questions. Why would Rafe stop you from killing that man if the guy was really so bad? Was he some kind of traitor?"

Noah shook his head. "I have no answers. I wish I could take back that day. I wish I could take back my ego, my determination, my ambition. I wish I had listened to your brother. I wish you'd gotten there just a second earlier or a second too late. I wish all kinds of things. But if you asked me to do it all over again, to protect you, or to ask Rafe those questions, I would always choose to protect you." He ducked his head. "But I know it doesn't matter how I feel about you. I could never deserve you. I promise that I'll continue to keep you safe until this threat is gone. And then you can have that life that you've always wanted. With no interference from me."

"Noah." She waited until he lifted his head. "What you do is not who you are. I don't know what the circumstances with Rafe really were. But I know you." The tears streamed down her cheeks. "I know you wouldn't have hurt him. Not on purpose. Especially not after what you've told me now."

She reached for his face. With the delicate touch of her fingertips along his cheekbone, he had no choice but to look at her.

God, she was so fucking beautiful.

Shameful

"Lucia, I'm not Prince Charming. I'm not some nice Italian boy who's going to marry you and give you lots of babies. I'm not."

"I'm glad you're not that guy. I don't want little Italian babies. All I want is you." She leaned forward, brushing her lips over his.

Chapter Six

Noah had never known you could taste love.

They'd kissed before but it hadn't been like this. Kissing Lucia was every dream he'd ever had made real. If it hadn't made him feel like a complete pussy he would have cried at the overwhelming waves of affection and acceptance he could feel emanating from her every caress. She was holding him in her arms and stroking his skin gently like he was something precious. Something that she treasured. How long had it been since anyone made him feel his existence made their life worth living? So long ago that he couldn't remember.

Maybe never.

"I love you so much, Noah. There were so many times I wished I could tell you how I felt."

Noah kept his face buried in the curve of her neck. She allowed him to stay there, her fingers stroking through his hair gently. He closed his eyes and inhaled the unique scent of Lucia. The scent of home.

"Why didn't you?" he finally asked.

"I was scared. You always treated me like a kid. If you'd rejected me, I think I would have died."

Her softly whispered words shook him. Although he wasn't the most demonstrative guy in the world, surely she'd been able to tell how she affected him. Could she not see how jealous he was when she gave those sweet smiles to anyone else? Maybe she hadn't noticed that he went on a rampage when her safety was threatened. It seemed insane that he could feel the things he did for Lucia and she would have no idea the entire time. There had been times he'd been sure his obsession with her was tattooed on his forehead for all to see.

"The only reason I tried to treat you like a little sister is because you're so young, Lucia. You needed time to grow up without some guy sniffing around your heels."

"I'm not that much younger than you," Lucia protested.

Although it was factually true, Noah snorted. Then he winced when she tugged his hair.

"I'm a grown woman, Noah. Even if you still see me as that stupid teenage girl who has no idea what's going on."

He pulled back slightly so he could see her eyes. "I've never thought you were stupid. What you are is … sheltered."

"And whose fault is that?" Her voice had softened slightly though.

"Mine. I acknowledge that with pride. Some things in this world should be sheltered because they're too precious to risk. You are too precious to risk, Lucia. A bright shining light in a world of darkness."

She let out a soft sigh and pressed a kiss to his forehead. "So are you. I know that you've had such a hard life, Noah. The things you've had to do to survive." Her voice wavered slightly. "But I understand. You've never wanted to hurt anyone. I know that with everything inside of me. And you deserve to be protected, too."

Then she was kissing him again and not with the gentle hesitancy he'd expected. She gripped his hair in both hands and devoured, sucking on his bottom lip with a carnal growl that sent most of his blood racing south. Noah groaned as he hardened instantly and Lucia purred when she felt his arousal. The little vixen had the nerve to slide her legs up and around his waist, squeezing tight and rocking against his length.

"Lucia," he breathed warningly.

"Yes. Did you need something?" She batted her eyelashes innocently. It was supposed to be innocent anyway but everything she did was sexy.

"Everything. I need everything from you."

Something snapped in him and he was suddenly intensely grateful they were already on the bed. They fell back onto the covers in a tangle of arms and legs. He couldn't get his mouth everywhere he wanted to at once and the urgency drove his need higher. Lucia bucked under him when he took a big mouthful of her breast, sucking hard through the fabric of her T-shirt.

"Need more," he growled and then pushed her shirt up and pulled the lacy cup of her bra down so he could get at what he wanted.

"Yes, that feels so good," Lucia whispered.

Her mouth fell open as his tongue swirled around the delicate point. Noah couldn't have stopped if he'd tried. He couldn't get enough of the taste of her skin. She whimpered his name several times before he gave her a break. When he pulled back, her nipple was hard and red as a cherry. Lucia's eyes followed the movement when he licked his lips.

"Noah! Take this off," she demanded.

He loved hearing the need in her voice, and her eyes glittered when he helped her sit up and pull the shirt off. At his first sight of her in nothing but panties and the lacy black bra, the swells of her generous breasts overflowing the cups, he almost broke down and begged right then and there. She was a goddess walking amongst mortals. Oblivious to his internal thoughts, Lucia pulled at the hem of his shirt.

"I'm the only one undressed. I'm feeling a little lonely over here."

"We can't have that." Noah yanked his T-shirt over his head and threw it on the floor.

Lucia sighed and wrapped her arms around his neck, pulling him down into her embrace.

"I really was lonely, you know. For so long all I've wanted was for you to see me. For you to let me love you and give you the family you've never had. I'll be your family, Noah. Me and, hopefully one day, our children. You'll never feel alone again."

His world stopped spinning and he pulled back to see her face. "Our kids?"

It shouldn't have been a surprise. He knew Lucia wanted children and a traditional family. Wasn't that why he'd hated watching her date so much? Because he'd known that one day she'd find some guy, marry him and pop out a few adorable babies. It had torn him up to imagine his Lucia round with another man's baby.

But the idea of fathering her children hit him like a

ton of bricks. He came from the streets and had very few
memories of his own father. What the hell did he know
about any of that? He'd seen so few functional relationships
that it was almost laughable to think he could suddenly be
husband and father material. Lucia needed a man who
could do both. He looked down at her all flushed and
glowing with love in his bed. What had he ever done to
deserve the love of a woman like this?

You don't deserve it, the insidious voice in the back of
his mind whispered. *She has no idea what you are truly
capable of.*

"Noah? What's wrong?"

He hadn't even realized he'd pulled away until she
spoke. Lucia crossed her arms, covering her breasts. Noah's
mind raced as he was assaulted with images of what the
future might hold— Lucia holding a beautiful baby with his
dark hair and her gray eyes. Lucia happy for a while until
she figured out that Noah would never be the man she
needed.

Lucia leaving him.

"Nothing. I need to check on things. Stay here." He
kissed her forehead softly when she started to speak. "I'll be
back."

He could feel her eyes on his back as he knelt to
grab his shirt off the floor. It felt like a laser drilling a hole
through him and it only made him move faster. He needed
to get away. Away from expectations and the love shining in

her eyes. He had a job to do. He would never be the man Lucia truly deserved but he could be the protector she needed. All this emotion was enough to make him forget what was truly important, keeping her safe. Emotion made you soft and he couldn't afford that.

Not with Lucia's life on the line.

Lucia watched with mounting fear as Noah dressed quickly and left the room. He'd moved stiffly while yanking his shirt back on, like he couldn't wait to get away from her.

She sighed.

With Noah the dance never ended. Anytime she thought she was making progress with him, something would happen to remind her that he wasn't just a guy. He was a complicated man with an extremely dark past. Despite everything they'd talked about today, she didn't fool herself into believing that he'd been completely honest. There were so many things about his past, especially his childhood, that he never discussed. She'd tried over the years to cajole information out of him.

Where had he lived up until his parents died?

Did he remember his life before then?

How had he survived being shuttled from foster

home to foster home?

So many questions. The only reason she even knew he'd been in foster care or that he was an orphan was because Rafe had told her once. Looking back, it was surprising that her secretive brother had shared even that much, but he'd been trying to make her understand why Noah was different from the boys she knew, despite being closer to her in age than he was to Rafe. No doubt her brother had thought it would turn her off and keep her away from Noah, but it had done the exact opposite.

Ever since she'd found out about his tragic beginnings, it had fostered a deep well of affection for the lost boy who'd become such a serious, brooding but protective man.

A man who was going to need more than a few *I love yous* to trust her. Lucia slid off the bed and found her shirt. After putting it on, she went into the en suite bathroom. Her hair was wild around her head but her eyes shined with a secret knowledge. She looked … happy.

It was true, she realized. Even though Noah had walked out, she'd gotten through to him. She'd shown him how she felt and received his love in return. Things weren't perfect but this was the happiest she'd ever been. Because now she knew Noah truly loved her, too.

After splashing water on her face, she patted her skin dry and secured her hair in a bun on top of her head. She walked back into the bedroom and then out to the hallway. The loft was always busy, so the sounds of voices didn't alarm her, not even when the voices turned into shouts. The guys who worked for Noah communicated the same way he did— loud and proud.

When she descended the stairs, Jonas stepped out of the kitchen. Just who she wanted to see. Lucia didn't know the whole story with Jonas but he definitely seemed to understand Noah. If anyone could shed some light on his behavior it was Jonas. Her second choice was Matthias, but she knew Noah thought of him as a kid. Plus she couldn't be sure he wouldn't go blabbing to Noah.

"Hey, can I talk to you for a minute?"

Jonas eyed her warily but followed her to the other side of the loft. There was a seldom-used sitting area with two couches separated by a glass-topped table. Lucia walked over to the tall windows looking out over the city. The view up here was simply breathtaking. The city looked like a maze of concrete and buildings. Jonas joined her at the window and took a sip from the mug of coffee he held.

"You've known Noah a long time, haven't you?"

Jonas nodded but didn't speak. Lucia smiled. These guys were all cut from the same cloth— suspicious, hesitant but loyal to the core. Jonas liked her, but he wouldn't do anything to betray his friend. It made her like him even more.

"Don't look so worried. I'm not asking you to tell me anything. I'm just happy that he has you as a friend. He deserves to have good people around him."

Jonas glanced back at the window. "He's hard to get

to know, but it's worth it. There have been so many times that guy has saved my ass."

"I'm sure you've done your share of saving, too."

He chuckled. "That I have. That is one crazy dude. You know I used to be a cop?"

"Sure I did." Lucia shook her head back and forth while she said it which made Jonas laugh.

Considering how closemouthed all these guys were, she was lucky just to know their names. Although, she could see Jonas as a cop. He was the type of guy who liked to follow the rules. He would have been one of the good ones, the kind in it for the right reasons, to serve and protect their community. The kind they needed.

"Well, there was a lot of corruption behind the scenes in my precinct. Noah got me out of a seriously fucked up situation and I never forgot it. When he offered me a job years later, it was a lifeline. I know you get frustrated with him but he's only trying to protect you. Funny thing is, I think you might be the one who can save him."

Lucia gulped, wishing with everything she had that it was true. "It's hard to hold someone close who doesn't know how to stay in one place. Noah isn't used to being loved."

Jonas was quiet for a minute and Lucia resisted the urge to beg him for more information. Although she did want his help, she'd never want to make him feel that he was compromising his loyalty to his friend. Sometimes that was the only thing you could count on. Now that she knew more about Noah's background, it was apparent why his friends were so important to him. Lucia was glad he had a whole team of people he could count on in his life. She loved him, and that was all she wanted for him. Even if she wished with all her heart that she could be one of those people he trusted implicitly.

"Don't give up on him. Be patient with him. He's only going to let you go so deep. Hell, he'll probably try to get away just because he thinks he's not good enough for you. Don't let him," Jonas finally said.

"I won't. I promise."

Lucia squeezed his arm before he walked away. In a way, she felt like she'd passed a test. Jonas had trusted her enough to tell her that and these guys, they didn't trust easily. But hopefully she'd shown them that she was trustworthy and, most importantly, that she loved them all. She would never do anything to hurt or compromise them.

Chapter Seven

The whole drive to Nonna's house, Lucia and Jonas sat in relatively companionable silence. Their earlier conversation had given her a lot to think about, and for that matter, so had Noah. When they reached her grandmother's house, Jonas parked then immediately busied himself with the football game on television. While he screamed about the Giants losing, Lucia took the time to question her grandmother.

Too bad Nonna was having none of that.

"Lucia, I've told you once if I've told you a hundred times, you sometimes have to let these things go. Sometimes you can't get answers."

Her grandmother stood at the stove stirring the sauce. The entire room smelled like rich tomatoes and spices. Lucia's stomach growled just from breathing the scent. Usually spending time in the kitchen with her grandmother was one of her favorite things to do. It was so relaxing to work side by side creating all of her favorite comfort foods. But today she got no joy from watching her Nonna work. Because she *knew* her grandmother was keeping things from her.

"I refuse to believe that, Nonna. This is my life, too. I've got these large, missing gaps that I think you can help me fill in. I want to be able to mourn Rafe properly." Why did everyone always meet her with resistance? Was it so wrong to want to know what had happened? To want to know the truth?

"He's gone, Lucia. You have to accept that."

Lucia threw up her hands. "I know he's gone, Nonna. I know nothing is going to bring him back, but these answers will help me put him to rest once and for all. I love Noah, but there is so much he hides from me. So much

Shameful

he's unwilling to show me."

Her grandmother sighed. "Sweetheart, maybe you weren't meant to see everything. You're only frustrating yourself. Men like to keep their secrets."

"I'm sorry, but I feel like that's a cop out, that notion that I just wasn't meant to know. I'm strong enough. Sooner or later everyone is going to have to see that." She lifted her gaze to meet her grandmother's while she was at the stove. "I know you are hiding things from me. And don't tell me that you've been squirreling money away for a rainy day. Don't tell me that over the years you've set something aside. That was a lot of money I found that day, Nonna. I know something is going on. And I want to know what."

At first, Lucia was convinced that her grandmother wasn't going to tell her. That once again she'd lie or evade. But then Nonna sighed and stopped stirring the sauce on the stove. She turned it down to a simmer then took a seat at the table.

"Ever since your parents died, you and Rafe lived with me. I'd always known that he was different. Sure he got in trouble, but there was a fierceness about him. A protectiveness. He wanted to do the right things. He wanted to look after you, look after me. He just didn't always choose the best roads to get there. Hit a little trouble here and there. Mostly kid stuff."

"Boys will be boys," Lucia offered helpfully. She hated that excuse. But her grandmother was old school.

Nonna nodded. "Yes. But your brother also had his own code of justice. When Bobby Nederlander down the street was bullying Jimmy Oates next door, calling him all kinds of horrid names, Rafe found the one way to make Bobby pay. He wanted to make sure he never did it again. It was public and harsh. But it got the point across."

Lucia frowned. She vaguely remembered, but it had been right after they came to live with Nonna. She was seven, maybe eight? But she remembered Bobby Nederlander. He'd been tied to a telephone post out front in just his boxers with 'I'm a coward' written on him in lipstick.

Someone also tied a feather boa around him, added a fuzzy hat, and clipped on his mother's earrings. The interesting thing was nobody had cut him down. He stayed like that for two and half hours until old Mr. Jamison down the street was heading for work. Everyone else was too scared to do it. It was as if there was some kind of code that everyone understood.

All Lucia knew was that after that day, Bobby had never bothered Jimmy again. Hell, Bobby kept the lowest profile ever. And he'd never said who tied him to the pole. It became this crazy urban legend, that there was some kind of bullying vigilante.

"I think I remember that. That was Rafe?"

Thinking about it, she remembered how after that day, somehow Jimmy had suddenly become all buddy-buddy with the jocks. Like he was under their protection or something. No doubt her brother's doing, though she didn't know it at the time.

Nonna smiled. "I know I shouldn't condone violence or vigilantism, but it made me feel proud. That even though your brother saw Jimmy next door as the annoying little kid, even though they had no friends in common, even though Jimmy was scrawny and not pleasant to be around, Rafe wanted justice and he fixed it the best way he knew how. And then he took care of him afterward like he was his. I'm still not entirely sure what he did to Bobby, but whatever it was put the kid back on the straight and narrow. He now works as a parole officer or something. Never had a spot of trouble after that."

Lucia wasn't entirely sure giving a kid like Bobby power was a good thing, but Nonna seemed to think it was. "I didn't know Rafe did that."

What else didn't she know about her brother? How much of himself had he kept hidden from her, from Nonna, from everyone?

Her grandmother nodded. "Noah is the same kind of person. From the moment Rafe brought him home and said he was the boy's mentor, I knew something was up. Noah had too many facets. He was too edgy, always looking like he was ready to run. The kind of look you get from a lifetime on the run, a lifetime of never being able to relax. Poor kid had no family. I'm not even entirely sure he was old enough to work at the security firm, but every other night or so Rafe would drag him home for dinner. What was I gonna do, not feed the kid? And then, he was always there, glued to your brother's hip. I finally started dragging the lot of you to Sunday Mass, trying to give all of you as much family time as I could."

Lucia sniffed back tears. "I needed that, Nonna. Noah knows what you did for him, too. He loves you."

"And just like your brother, he has a firm idea of justice and what's right. When that money started to turn up six years ago, I knew it was him, seeing that we were taken care of. He knew if he tried to give it to me outright, I wouldn't take it. So he gave it to me in a way that I couldn't deny it. Pure hard cash. He's been sending it to me for years. Once a month, on the first, a few thousand dollars. It helped with the extras, especially when you were younger. I wouldn't have been able to afford the Catholic school that I sent you to in high school on my own. The money helped a lot."

Lucia blinked back her shock. "I had no idea. Nonna, if you need money—"

Her grandmother waved her off. "No, no, no. It's not that I needed money. Because we would've figured something out. You would've gone to that school on a scholarship, no doubt. But it was about the extras. So that I could get you a nice prom dress instead of having to make it for you. So that when your school took an international trip, I could afford to send you. That money made all the difference. And Noah saw to it. And I don't want to know where the money came from or how he went about it. But I know I can count on it. And I know he does it because he loves us. Although, I know he can't always find the words."

Lucia hugged herself tight, rocking back and forth. For six years, Noah had helped look after her grandmother. Something she'd been trying to do but had been unsuccessful at thus far. He'd looked after her and made sure she hadn't wanted for anything. He looked after Lucia, too. Even when she wanted to dislike him. Like with her rent. Like now. Her heart squeezed. How could he not see how good he was?

"Nonna, has Noah ever said where the money comes from? He only started Blake Security four years ago. What was he doing for money before then?"

Her grandmother lowered her lashes. "I have learned over the years, when people do good, sometimes it's best not to ask how or why. Just accept it and be grateful."

Lucia wished she could do that. Turn the other cheek and not ask questions. But she couldn't. All she wanted to do was understand Noah. And for that, she was going to need some answers.

Lucia wished the afternoon with Nonna had given her more insight. Well, she'd gotten a few answers to her brother's past. And she knew how long Noah had been looking out for them. Nonna hadn't said it directly, but her grandmother was likely assuming he hadn't gotten the money legitimately. Thankfully she'd never guess the truth. She knew what he was capable of but she didn't want him hiding anymore. Lucia didn't care who he'd been or what he'd done, she knew who Noah *really* was.

Despite all that, she was still not completely ready to accept this new version of Rafe. She couldn't bring herself to believe that part. It was difficult after having one image of him her whole life to suddenly realign all those facts into a new picture.

When Jonas brought her back to the office, she gave him a tight hug and told him she was sorry about the Giants. Of course that made him moan and grumble as he walked toward the kitchen to rustle up some food. As it was Sunday, it was really only her, Matthias, and Jonas around.

Matthias had been making himself scarce. Noah was God knew where. As she headed back to her room, she passed Noah's office and hesitated.

No. You can't go in there. Snooping is not going to get you anything you want.

Yeah, that and Noah would be *pissed*. But seeing as he refused to tell her anything, seeing as she didn't have any answers, this might be the only way. At least that was the lie she told herself. Justifications were a funny thing.

Looking around, she noted that Matthias and Jonas were still hanging around the kitchen. That meant they wouldn't see her on the cameras. At least not yet.

Quickly, she tiptoed into Noah's office, closing the glass door behind her. She had no idea what she was looking for. The office was stark at best. Massive glass table. Modern leather chairs, steel, chrome, glass. Eggshell walls. No pictures. A stark, bleak canvas. That was Noah. She always wondered how he could possibly work in here. It just felt so empty. Maybe that was how he felt all the time. She had no idea.

Her only option was to check the bookshelves. She did it meticulously, putting each book back exactly as she found them. *What do you think you're going to find?* She had no idea. Hell, she had no idea what she was even looking for. Just some kind of clue. Something labeled 'Rafe and Noah's secret redacted file' here, but she doubted she'd get that lucky. She just had a feeling that finding answers about Noah would help her find some answers about Rafe.

In the end it didn't matter what she searched, since Noah's office was as impenetrable as the man himself. His laptop was password protected, and most of the drawers in his desk were locked. Except for one. The top one. Inside, she found a picture of him and her, at the beach. It was taken maybe last year. There was no frame. Just the picture. He'd picked her up and had her tossed over his shoulder. She was kicking frantically, trying to get him to let go of her. Of course, they were both laughing like loons. She didn't even know he had a picture of that day.

And underneath the picture, she found a friendship

bracelet. The strings were pink and green, purple and yellow. She remembered exactly when she'd made it. Summer camp when she was thirteen. When she returned home, everyone still treated her like she was a kid, but not Noah. He talked to her, asked her questions. Wanted to really know about her. She had given it to him, because for a thirteen-year-old girl, that was the height of friendship. Someone who would actually listen to you and didn't overlook you because you were a child. He'd kept this all these years? She fingered the cotton delicately when a voice startled her out of her reverie.

"I must've lost my shit when you gave it to me."

Lucia dropped the bracelet and the photo. "Noah, I —"

He crossed his arms and leaned in the doorframe. "You were just what? Doing a little light snooping?"

"Sorry. I should never have—" She looked down at her hands. "I shouldn't have invaded your privacy. I know. But, since that's what you do to me …" She shrugged. "Turnabout's fair play."

Noah stayed in the doorframe. Arms crossed, gorgeous face turned down into a scowl. "No one had ever given me anything before. Not really. Not anything meaningful. And you were just a kid. Thirteen, fourteen? You gave me that bracelet. I still remember asking you what it was for, and you said it was for friendship."

She smiled at the memory. "I don't think I ever saw you without it after that."

Shameful

Noah licked his lips even as he shifted his gaze downward. "I didn't take it off. If you look at it closely, you'll see there's blood on it. I stopped wearing it after that day."

Lucia's bottom lip quivered. "Noah. I'm sorry."

He left the doorway then and strode toward her. Anyone else would have been scared. He moved like an animal on the prowl. But Lucia wasn't going to run. He didn't scare her. She shoved the drawer closed and came around the desk to meet him halfway.

"You shouldn't be sticking your nose where it doesn't belong," he growled low.

"I know. I'm sorry, but after we talked you shut down on me. I'm just trying to know you. Know something about you that's real and not an illusion, not a charade, and not a lie. Since you won't talk to me, I'm—" She shook her head. "No. I shouldn't have snooped. It was invasive. Sorry."

She lifted her head and met his gaze. His eyes were stormy as he gazed into hers. "Lucia, God, what are you doing to me?"

And then his lips crashed over hers. Automatically Lucia's arms wrapped around his neck and with a low growl, Noah lifted her and placed her on the edge of the desk. His tongue delved in and stroked against hers, teasing, drawing a response out of her. He tasted like coffee, and mint, and something spicy. And she loved it. She wanted more.

He tried to pull back, but she locked her legs around him and tightened her arms. Logically, she knew she couldn't hold him if he wanted to go. But it didn't stop her from trying. Noah whispered against her lips. "I couldn't stay away from you if I tried."

"Then why are you trying?" she whispered.

"Because I know the fire will consume us."

He delved back in with his tongue, licking into her mouth, making her shudder. Her body wanted the things that he silently promised; things dark and delicious that made her feel desperate. When he slid his hands up under her top skimming his thumbs along the edges of her ribs, she gasped and arched her back into the caress. He dragged his kisses along her jaw, her neck, all the while his hands skimmed rib over rib, and finally just under her breasts.

And Lucia knew that this was what she wanted. *He* was what she wanted. She just needed to convince him that he wanted to keep her.

He drew back. "Be sure, Lucia. Because, if I have you, I'm never letting you go."

She met his gaze directly. "I'm sure, Noah. I love you."

Chapter Eight

Noah picked her up, his control gone. When their lips met, it was a hard mesh of lips and teeth and hot panting breaths. There was something in the back of his head screaming at him to treat her gently. Not to unleash the animalistic urge to take, bite, and ravage. But Lucia didn't shrink away as he kissed his way across her neck to take the lobe of her ear between his teeth. No, she moaned and dug her delicate fingers into his shoulders, the sharp bites of pain just sending his already crazed desire through the roof.

"You weren't supposed to know," he rasped in between hot, suctioning kisses down her collarbone.

"Know what?" She squeaked when he set her down on top of the desk. Her eyes were slightly unfocused and her lips were red and swollen.

Noah grunted, pleased by the evidence of her desire. He wanted to see it all over her. She should always look this way, flushed and satisfied.

"You weren't supposed to know how long I've wanted you. I was supposed to be your protector, and I tried so hard to stay away. Not to want you."

His words seemed to please her because her lips curled into a devious smile. "You didn't have to stay away."

"I did, hell, I probably still should. But I've tried that and it doesn't work. I'm drawn to you and nothing is keeping me away now. You're mine."

Noah loved how she clung to him, like she couldn't get enough of the feel of his skin. Her touch made him feel primal, like he'd kill anything that ever threatened her. He picked her up, enjoying the feel of her curvy little ass in his hands. Lucia was petite but lush in all the right places. He could spend an entire night just worshipping the perfect globes of her ass.

She moaned as he squeezed the soft flesh, hefting her higher so he didn't have to break the kiss. If it were possible, he'd have his hands and lips all over every inch of her skin simultaneously. Desire rode him hard, making him crazed to do it all, touch it all, have it all at once.

"You make me so fucking crazy," he growled, charmed when she giggled and clamped her legs around his waist.

"I haven't even done anything." Lucia pulled his head down and peppered kisses all over his face.

Goddamn, she was so sweet. She touched him gently and each one of those delicate little touches made him hard as stone. He clenched his teeth, trying to keep himself in check. As much as he wanted to just throw her down on this desk and fuck her hard, he needed to be gentle with her. Careful.

Lucia seemed to have different ideas because she bit his bottom lip before soothing the hurt with her tongue. His eyes flew open and their gazes locked and held. In that moment Noah saw everything in her eyes. This woman was the one he'd never dared hope to wish for, the other half of his broken soul and the one person who would love him despite his past.

She seemed to sense the importance of the moment also because her hands tightened around his neck.

"Noah, I need you. Right now." Her words were

strangled before her mouth was on his and she yanked at the front of his shirt.

Dimly, he heard the soft clatter of buttons hitting the floor but it was swallowed by the roaring in his ears. *She needs me*. There was nothing she could have said that would have aroused him more than that.

They were a blur of movements as they wrestled to get out of their clothes. Noah moaned aloud when her teeth sank into the bare skin of his shoulder. Shocked that she would actually bite him, he growled and shoved everything on the desk to the floor.

"Noah, your laptop!"

Lucia looked up at him in surprise as he stretched her out over the surface of the desk. Most of her clothes had been shed and littered the floor at his feet except for a pair of sheer black panties. Her nipples tightened under his gaze, the perfect rose points drawing his attention like beacons. His mouth watered just looking at her.

"I'll buy another fucking laptop."

Then he leaned over her and used his teeth to nip at those damn candy-colored nipples. How could any woman be this sweet? He'd been with a lot of women, probably way too many, and no one had ever made him feel like this. Crazed to touch, taste and stroke every inch. It wasn't just for his own pleasure either but he wanted to drive her crazy and treat her the way she deserved. He *needed* to hear Lucia scream his name. Needed it like he needed his next breath.

When he moved to kiss her belly button she giggled,

her torso twisting away from him. She gripped his hair as if to stop him, but of course that only made the game more fun.

"Noah, stop teasing."

"Never, princess. I plan on teasing you until you barely know your own name."

Her sigh hit his ears just as he buried his face between her thighs. The sigh turned into a moan as he nuzzled the soft curls on her mound. He liked the fact that she didn't shave or wax it bare completely. All the women he'd been with before had been like smooth, plastic Barbies between their legs. They'd made noises calculated to sound sexy, moved their gym-toned bodies to pose for him and said what they thought he wanted to hear.

But none of that shit had ever mattered.

Lucia was real; she didn't know how to be anything but who she was and he never wanted her to learn. Nothing about her was calculated or fake. He realized now that she was the one person who'd always loved him for absolutely no reason at all.

"You are perfect, Lucia. Absolutely fucking perfect." Noah punctuated each word with a kiss, licking deeper and harder until she was moaning wildly. "That's it, just let go for me, beautiful."

Lucia's fingers tangled in his hair until he was sure he'd have a bald spot. Not that he cared. It was a small price to pay for the honor of having his tongue deep in the sweetest pussy he'd ever had.

When she came, her grip tightened and she let out a soft, keening cry. Her thighs clenched around his face and Noah had to restrain himself from beating his chest. When he finally lifted his head, she was flushed and dazed, watching him with sleepy gray eyes.

"Don't check out on me yet, baby."

That seemed to spark something in her because the sassy look he loved came back to her eyes.

"Check out? Can't a girl take a breath?"

She sat up then and put her arms around his neck. He kissed her, allowing her to taste herself on his lips. Lucia moaned and then wrapped her legs around his waist.

"Are you sure you aren't checking out, old man?"

Noah chuckled at the familiar joke. He'd never known sex could be this much fun. But then again, Lucia made everything fun.

"You've almost worn this old man out. But not quite. Hold on to me."

She squealed when he lifted her and carried her to the wall behind his desk. With her legs locked around his waist, she was at the perfect height for—

"Oh my god," Lucia moaned as he slid inside in one smooth stroke. Her head fell back against the wall with a thump. The look on her face was pure ecstasy.

He would have taken more time to appreciate the view if he wasn't so consumed by the sensation of being wrapped up in her. It was like having his dick encased in heaven and he didn't want to miss a moment. He clenched his teeth against the urge to come immediately. Lucia was moaning and gyrating in his arms, making his job even harder. Then she clamped her arms around his neck and pulled his mouth to hers.

And the battle was lost.

He thrust harder and harder, ignoring the voice in the back of his head screaming for him to be gentle. She was so open, her soft wet flesh enveloping him over and over until she tensed and smacked his shoulder, tears streaming down her face.

"Fuck, I can't take it," Noah growled.

Lucia lifted her head. "Yes, come with me."

He gave up the fight then and succumbed to the most intense pleasure he'd ever experienced. Having her eyes on him the whole time made it even more intense because he felt like he was inside her in every way, body and soul. When the last shudder of pleasure left him, Noah wasn't sure how he managed to remain upright. The wall behind them was the only reason they weren't both flat on their asses right then because his legs felt like jelly.

Suddenly he heard the muted sound of clapping. His head whipped around and he saw Oskar right outside his office wearing a big grin and clapping like a madman. Noah cursed. He hadn't remembered to frost the windows in his office so they were still visible to everyone.

"Thanks for the free show!" Oskar yelled and then gave them both a big thumbs-up.

Lucia groaned and then buried her head in his shoulder. When her shoulders started shaking Noah saw red. He would pound Oskar for embarrassing her later.

"Don't cry, sweetheart. I'm sorry about the windows. I forgot—" He stopped abruptly when she lifted her head and he saw that she wasn't crying. The little brat had the nerve to be laughing.

"Noah, I'm not the one who gave him the show. Your naked ass is what everyone has been looking at the whole time!" She broke off into another fit of giggles that instantly made everything right in the world again.

Lucia woke while he was carrying her up the stairs. She smiled and turned her head into Noah's chest. It was fascinating to observe him when he wasn't aware. Her warrior. That was what it felt like. Maybe it was shallow but she couldn't deny it was insanely sexy the way he insisted on picking her up all the time. How was she supposed to resist a guy who treated her like the most precious thing in the world? She imagined this was what the queens of old had felt like being protected by knights who'd pledged their lives.

Shameful

Lucia sobered slightly at the thought that Noah truly would sacrifice his life for her. That was the last thing she wanted. In a perfect world, she imagined them spending decades together in the future, growing old and cranky together. He'd annoy her with his overbearing nature and she'd drive him crazy by defying him at every turn.

And she'd love him until the day she died.

"Sleep, princess." Noah tucked her under the covers and smoothed the hair back from her face.

Lucia scooted over and held the covers open. "Not unless you come, too?"

He hesitated, glancing over his shoulder at the open door. The muted hum of voices floated up from the floor below. Lucia sighed. Having her around was probably putting a huge strain on Noah's workload because he obviously wasn't used to taking meals or retiring at a decent hour. But she couldn't help herself. She wanted more of him; no, *needed* more of him. It felt like nothing too bad could happen if he was there. She didn't mean to use him as the human equivalent of a blankie, but there was no denying that his presence comforted her.

"Okay, let me just check on a few things."

He leaned down and pressed a kiss to her forehead before walking back out, pulling the door closed behind him.

Lucia rolled over to face the window. He was probably hoping that she'd fall asleep in the meantime so he could get back to work. Tears pricked at the corners of her eyes. She didn't know what to do with all these new feelings. Noah had always been there as a part of her life, but he'd never been the center of it. Their new relationship had thrown her completely off balance, and it was scary to be out here on the limb dangling all alone. Noah said that he loved her, but she didn't know if it meant the same thing to him as it did to her. Lucia hated to feel so needy, but truthfully, she had to acknowledge that she'd always needed Noah. It was only recently that she'd been able to openly admit it and embrace the way he made her feel.

It was probably way too much to hope that he felt the same way.

She wasn't sure how much time passed before the door opened, the hum of voices getting louder and then cutting off again when the door closed. Lucia squeezed her eyes closed, as if it would keep Noah from seeing how upset she was. The bed dipped slightly under his weight, and she squeaked when he grabbed her and dragged her against him.

"You've never been able to fake sleep, Lu. Not even when you were a kid."

Lucia huffed out a breath and rolled over to face him. His eyes traced over her face, taking in the tear trails and her no doubt puffy eyes, but he didn't say anything. Not that he needed to. All she needed was what she had right now—Noah holding her close and making everything better.

Shameful

"I'm glad you're here." Lucia rested her head on his chest, lulled by the steady thump of his heart under her cheek. She counted the beats, imagining that each one beat to the rhythm of his love for her.

"Me too. I love having you in my bed. This is where you belong."

Lucia wrapped an arm around his waist and hugged him tighter. Every inch of him was covered in muscle, but somehow he still made a very comfortable pillow. She had to stop herself from giggling at the thought of his reaction to being called cuddly. Noah was totally the alpha male, aggressive, hear-me-roar type. He'd probably hate being considered sensitive in any way.

"What are you giggling about down there?"

"Nothing," Lucia lied. "Just thinking about everything. We've known each other so long that it feels like you've always been in my life."

He shrugged, the movement displacing her from his chest slightly. She sat up and looked at him in the darkness. Even in the dark room, his eyes glowed with intensity. She had no doubt that even now, when he appeared to be relaxing, he was on alert for anything that might pose a threat. He'd been taking care of her and Nonna for years now. But who took care of him? When did he get to relax?

It was a telling thought that she'd never considered that before. She'd been more than content to live her life unaware, happy in the world that Noah made safe for her without ever thinking of the things he must have sacrificed to keep her that way. It shamed her that she'd been so oblivious for so many years. Despite being the ultra-capable, alpha-male, badass type, she liked to think that someone was looking out for Noah, too.

"I was just thinking about how you've been so amazing, always being there for me and Nonna over the years."

"That's no hardship, Lu. I want to be there for you two. You're my family."

"I know. But I'm just grateful that you feel that way. Nonna doesn't let people help her easily, but she told me about the money you've been sending her every month. I know she's too stubborn to thank you so I'll do it. Thank you for taking such good care of us."

She leaned down and hugged him again. He was stiff against her for a long moment before he slowly relaxed. She knew it was hard for him to show affection; it just wasn't something he was used to. Everything she'd learned about his past made her want to shower him in love and show him that he was worthy of it. He might not be used to this kind of attention, but she would continue to show him with her actions how much he meant to her.

"Nonna is stubborn. So … what has she been doing with the money?"

Lucia shrugged. "She says she's saving it for a rainy day. But it's not like she'll ever need it. I saw that you paid her hospital bill, too. You're so good to us, Noah."

He pulled her tighter and kissed the top of her head. "You deserve everything in the world. Now go to sleep. I know you're tired."

"No, I'm not," she protested but the words were broken by a huge yawn. Her eyes closed involuntarily and once they were closed, it was hard to open them again.

Noah's husky chuckle warmed her. It was so nice to hear him laughing instead of being so serious for a change. After everything they'd gone through together, all the tragedy, Lucia decided then and there that she would bring laughter back into his life.

"Goodnight, princess."

It was the last thing she heard before she dropped off into sleep.

Chapter Nine

Noah didn't want to leave Lucia's bed again. Not after the last time. But he couldn't sleep. However, if he stayed he'd only wake her, and then neither one of them would get any sleep. Not that he minded, but she needed rest. It had been a long few days, and she was running on nothing but adrenaline.

She hadn't been sleeping well lately, but given that

last orgasm, he hoped she'd be out for hours. Unless he was losing his touch. Though given her cries of "Oh my God, Noah … There, right there … Please oh God, yeah," he doubted it. With a smirk, he dragged on pajama bottoms that he found in the back of his drawer. When was the last time he put on pajama bottoms?

Quietly, he padded out of his room, gently closing the door behind him. His first stop was the tech room. He doubted Matthias was asleep. The kid barely ever slept. Too many nightmares, Noah guessed. What Noah wasn't sure of was whether it was stuff from his life before or the things that ORUS asked him to do that kept the kid up. Anyway, if Noah didn't live with him he would have never known he barely got more than three or four hours a night. Occasionally he'd take a catnap, but somehow the kid was always alert, hyperaware, ready to run.

As expected, he found Matthias in front of a couple dozen monitors. Most of the computer screens were security feeds. Places that needed watching. Their own building. Lucia's building. A couple of clients' locations. The other monitors displayed code. Lines and lines of code. Noah learned from experience, that it was never a good idea to ask exactly what Matthias was working on. He would either go into extreme detail, boring you with the nuances of every one and zero, or he'd tell you exactly what he was doing, which occasionally would make your hair stand on end. Especially when it dealt with nuclear codes. Noah shuddered.

He hated to think of just how many governments Matthias could fuck with just because he felt like it. Good thing he was one of the good guys. *Good thing you saved him.*

"Kid, need any help?"

Matthias spun around, dragging an earbud out of his ear, the other hand in his lap, wrapped around the muzzle of his gun. "Fuck, Noah. You startled the shit out of me."

Noah held his hands up. "Easy does it, kid. You could hurt someone with that."

For a long moment, the guy gave him a flat stare. Completely dead eyes, as if he were running through the scenarios. That was the shit that scared Noah. For a moment in time, he thought he had lost his friend. And then Matthias blinked. He was coming back to himself. His hand gently eased off of the gun. "Sorry. I thought you guys were asleep. I'm just edgy after the fashion show."

Noah nodded and gently eased his hands down. "You know, we didn't talk about it. After you brought her back, we didn't —"

Matthias shook his head. "I'm fine."

Noah sighed. "I know you're fine, but I need to know if you're tight. I know that day probably triggered a whole bunch of bad shit for you. I'm sorry I put you in that position."

Matthias looked down at the gun in his lap. "I had a job to do. I didn't even think twice. That's the shit that scares me. It was like an instinct. Every goddamn move, pure instinct. I was ready and willing and wanting to rip the head off of whoever walked through the door. I was *disappointed* that there wasn't something bad on the other side. I *wanted* to kill something." He picked up the gun and put it on his desk. "So yeah, I'm fine. But maybe not tight."

Shit. He had to get the shrink. "Okay. I hear you. I'm feeling like I shouldn't have given you that assignment so soon after we talked to the FBI."

"No. We're running ourselves ragged here. I need to pull my weight. Even if it means that you have to pull the trigger. I'll try not to get too lost. Besides, it was Lucia. Maybe that's why I didn't blink. I knew I had to protect her."

Noah's gut curled. He knew the kid had a crush but didn't that sound vaguely like love? "Listen, kid, I know how you feel about—"

Matthias shook his head. "I'm good. You love her. And she loves you. Besides, she and I were only ever going to be friends. I know it's not like that."

Damn straight it wasn't. Every one of Noah's territorial instincts had already been triggered having her around all the guys. Probably why he was just about ready to fuck her on every flat surface of his office as much as he could. But he didn't say that out loud. "Good," he managed.

Matthias smirked and began turning the chair around. "Besides, given how loud she is, the whole office heard she's pretty much yours."

Motherfucker. They'd heard her. Every damn word. "You guys need to learn to shut your fucking ears off."

Matthias lifted his brow. "Can't. You pay me to watch and listen to everything. Eyes and ears, bruv. And unfortunately I got more than an eyeful. And earful."

They'd been in his office. Sure Oskar had gotten a view, but how had Matthias? "You didn't see shit."

Matthias glanced over his shoulder and winced. "Next time, boss, you might want to use the privacy glass and remember I've got cameras in every corridor. Everyone pretty much stayed in the conference room until you guys, uh, finished. Except Oskar of course. He was unlucky enough to come in after you two uh … commenced."

Noah cursed. "You're saying all of you guys got a good look at Lucia's ass?"

Matthias shook his head quickly. "No, unfortunately, we all got a good view of *your* ass." He shuddered. "I'd rather not have to look again."

Noah shook his head and laughed. "Sorry. Privacy glass. Got it."

"Thanks. I know the only reason you're not waking up half of this building with her screams is because you need something."

Damn. This was going to be tricky. With her here, his whole crew was going to get an eyeful of her at some point. *You have to figure out how to mitigate that.* But that was another problem for another day. Right now he had a very specific problem. "Okay, so Lucia went to see her grandmother today. Nonna said she's been getting money for years. Since Rafe died. Cash in her mailbox, once a month or so. Could be at night or during the day when she's out. But not just a little money. A few thousand. Maybe five."

Matthias frowned. "That's well over a hundred grand for the year."

"I know. And the kicker is she thinks I've been sending her that money."

"You're shitting me right?"

Noah shook his head. "I swear. Not shitting you. I need to find out where the fuck that money is coming from."

Matthias tapped away on one of his keyboards. "And it started showing up after Rafe was gone?"

Noah nodded. "According to Lucia, and what Nonna told her, as soon as Rafe died, the money turned up. Now, if it was an electronic transfer or something, I would say that was Rafe's set up. Then when he died, all of his money would go straight to her. Hell, that's my set up. But this is something else. It's coming in cash to her door."

Matthias shrugged. "Maybe Rafe had someone set up to bring it to her."

Noah didn't buy it. "Yeah, but if he did, that would be me. Nonna practically raised me to adulthood. I'd be the one sending her money. Hell, I do send her money. Not as much as that, but still every month. I take it over when we do Sunday dinner. She never says a word." He ran his hand through his hair. "I need you to find out where the money's coming from. While you're at it, find out what happened to Rafe's accounts. I knew that man better than I would know my own brother. He would've wanted Nonna and Lucia taken care of. Why hasn't his money from ORUS been coming back? That's a good place to start."

Matthias nodded as he started typing frantically. "If there's a trail to be found, I'll find it. If worse comes to worst, we put a man on her house, round-the-clock, and find out how that money is being delivered, and by whom."

Noah heard Lucia softly calling for him. He turned his attention briefly to Matthias. "Let me know when you find something." He didn't wait for Matthias to answer before he was already heading back to the bedroom. Apparently Lucia's nightmares were too much for her to sleep, too. Good thing he knew exactly how to help get her back to sleep.

Lucia stretched gloriously. Noah Blake knew how to deliver one hell of a wake-up call. Jesus, she may not be able to move her legs ever. She was certain they didn't work properly.

After he'd stretched over her that morning, intent

on giving her the wake-up call to end all wake-up calls, he'd told her to join him in the shower. Lord knew she would have, but she could barely sit up, let alone stand.

And if she knew Noah, no way would he have her in there *just* to shower. Oh, it might start innocently enough. A little harmless soaping of her back here, a little rinsing of her breasts there. It was a slippery slope with that man. He really was shameless.

The things that man could do with his hands. And his mouth. Not to mention his dick. *Wow*. She'd never even known it could be like this with someone. Sure, she'd had a feeling they could be explosive, but there was no anticipating Noah Blake. The problem was now that she knew he wanted her, would she ever be able to stop? The man was addictive. And that thing, the fluttering he did just when she hovered on the edge of oblivion … Holy hell. More than once she'd been sure he was trying to kill her with sex. There were worse ways to go than death by orgasm.

And truth be told, she was tempted to throw the covers off and join him as he suggested. She wanted to run the soap all over his body. It didn't take much before her imagination was running away with her. If she could move, she *would* join him. She would help soap his back and his abs. Because *obviously* he would need help washing his abs. There were so many of them, after all.

And of course she'd wash other things too. She'd never admit it to him, but she loved being able to snap his control. It always gave her a rush of feminine power that she could bring a man like Noah to his knees. And she wanted to learn all the ways to do just that. It made her wish she'd brought along the box of lingerie, toys, and videos she'd gotten from that bachelorette party.

While she was mulling the possibility of Noah allowing her back into her apartment to retrieve it, her phone rang. Unwilling to get out of bed into the chilly morning air, she wiggled sideways and leaned over the side of the bed to pick up her purse and drag her phone out. The number was unknown so she didn't answer at first but then wondered if it might be important.

"Hello?"

"Lucia?"

It took a moment before she could place the slightly familiar voice. "*Brent*? Where are you?"

"It's better that I don't tell you." His voice was garbled for a moment, and she strained to hear. "Lucia, listen to me. You're in danger."

Wait, how did he know that? Did he know about the attack? "Brent, what do you mean? How did you know? It only just happened. Besides, I thought that you were out of this whole thing. I thought you had managed to run."

He coughed. "I didn't run far enough. Listen. Maybe I did something stupid, but after I saw you I started to poke around some more. I think I asked the wrong kind of questions. Because there's been a team following me since

I left New York. I should keep moving, but I needed to tell you."

Why would he do that? Why would he risk his life, his freedom, for hers? That was madness. "Tell me what?"

"Listen, not over the phone. It's too dangerous. But there are people trying to hurt you. There are people trying to kill you. I made a mistake. I don't want you to as well. You need to get out of town, too."

She sat up, wrapping her arms around herself. "What mistakes did you make? You have to give me more to go on. You can't just tell me to leave town. You don't understand. My whole life is here."

"Lucia, this is serious!"

"I know, please don't think I'm not taking it seriously. I know that someone is after me, but Noah and his team have told me they'll look into it. I trust him to keep me safe. I don't want to run away. You shouldn't have to run away either."

There was a long pause on the phone. Then he spoke, his voice low. "Lucia, you don't get it. You're going up against the mafia."

She gasped. "What do you mean mafia? Who?"

Brent shushed her. "I don't know if they can tap the line you're on, but we can't talk about this openly. Look, I'm coming back to the city. Can you meet me?"

Was he insane? There was no way in hell Noah was letting her out of his sight. Unfortunately, Noah also wasn't going to tell her a damn thing about who was after her. If she wanted some information, she was going to have to dig it out on her own. And Brent obviously knew something she didn't.

But the real trick would be getting away. For her own safety, Noah was never going to let her out of his sight. One of the guys was always with her. Maybe it was time to call JJ. She'd have a way.

"Okay look. I'll meet you. You name the place, we'll come and you have to let Noah help you. This is what his team does. He can keep you safe. He can hide you a damn sight better than you're hiding yourself right now."

"No. He can't. And as a matter-of-fact, I think you should stay away from him. I don't have all the pieces, but I think your boyfriend knows more about this than he's telling you. Look, we can't talk on the phone. I'll give you all the information when I see you. Come alone. I'll text you the location."

She bit her bottom lip. She'd promised Noah that she was going to let him and his guys deal with this. But if Brent would only talk to her, that's just the way it was. Besides, she would be cautious. She wasn't going to lose this opportunity to get more information.

"Fine. Text me the address. I'll be there."

"Okay but remember—Come alone. I don't trust that guy. You may think he's on the up and up but you need to be careful. We all do."

Chapter Ten

Noah was going to kill her. Kill her dead. But only after he gave her that disappointed look he gave her when she didn't trust him. *He's going to great lengths to protect you and this is how you betray him?* Lucia tried to shove that thought to the back of her mind.

She battled back the guilt that kept trying to surface as she patted down the blond wig that hid her dark hair. In the next stall, she could hear JJ changing into the clothes that Lucia had been wearing. If all went according to plan, she would leave the restroom dressed like JJ and no one would be the wiser. *Except you. You will be the wiser. You will know that you're lying.*

Oskar was going to be pissed if he figured out what she was up to, but she honestly couldn't think of anything else to do. She was all out of options and Brent was offering her a lifeline. She had to take it.

She pulled out her phone and looked at the text message she'd received from Brent earlier in the day. It had been such a surprise to hear from him since she'd thought he'd already left town. But from the tone of his message, he had something really important to share. Considering the type of information he'd already given her, she figured it was worth her while to see him.

Even if that meant ditching her bodyguard. Oskar was family now. She felt terrible … except she didn't. As bad as she felt, she knew what was at stake.

"Are you ready?" JJ whispered. There was no one else in the restroom so her voice was audible almost as if they were in the same stall.

Lucia yanked up the skinny jeans that didn't want to cover her ass. JJ was a lot taller so she'd had to roll up the bottoms slightly. Hopefully once she put on JJ's hat over the wig and the huge handbag, it wouldn't be as noticeable that she'd lost a few inches in height. Or that she didn't have her best friend's characteristic swagger and flair.

It wasn't too late. She could still stop this. She could still go back and let Noah handle this. *But can you really?* She knew Noah would protect her from everything that he could. But she had to do this. This was for Rafe. She *needed* these answers. "As ready as I'll ever be."

She opened the stall and walked out and instantly laughed at the sight of JJ in Lucia's blouse and too-big jeans. Her friend wasn't as busty so the blouse gaped quite a bit while the jeans were baggy and way too short.

"Don't you dare laugh!"

Lucia clamped her lips shut. "Thank you for this. Just walk fast and then go in the bathroom of the coffee shop. I'll tell Oskar later that I had diarrhea or something."

JJ's eyes went wide, and she stifled a laugh. "Okay that's way TMI. But it will definitely work. If not, tell him you have your period. No guy is going to ask for details at that point."

JJ handed over her large purse and waited while Lucia took out her phone from her own bag. Once she had a chance to see Brent, they'd meet back up at the coffee shop and switch their clothes back.

"Okay let's go. Hopefully He-Man out there won't get too close otherwise the jig is up."

Lucia blew out a breath and waited while JJ went

out first. They were hoping that Oskar would follow JJ for a while, giving Lucia time to slip out. And lovely as he was, he did just as expected. After all Lucia was the target, she was the one who someone wanted to hurt. Of course Oskar followed Noah's orders. She almost felt bad for how much shit he'd catch if anything happened to her today, but she couldn't think about that now.

After two minutes, Lucia opened the door and walked quickly with her head down. She didn't see any sign of Oskar, so she rushed out onto the sidewalk. It wasn't easy to navigate all the people rushing by with her head down but she didn't want to chance being seen in case Oskar was still hanging around. All she needed was a ten-minute window to get the information she needed. Her breath came fast as she approached where Brent had agreed to meet her.

She opened the door to the small restaurant and looked around the dim interior. There was a table free near the window so she slid into the seat and put JJ's oversized bag on her lap. After a few minutes, she started to wonder if she'd made a mistake. Noah was going to be pissed if he found out and really, how had she thought that she'd be able to pull this off? She was hardly a super-spy.

Just when she was contemplating getting up and leaving, someone pulled out the chair across from her and sat down. Brent looked up from under the hoodie he was wearing.

"Hey." She didn't know what else to say considering how bad he looked.

Shameful

Brent was a pretty good-looking guy but now he had large bags under his eyes and his skin was sallow. He hadn't shaved in days, if not more. And he'd lost weight. How was that even possible? If she hadn't just seen him a few weeks ago, she wouldn't believe it was the same person. This guy was a wrecked facsimile of that version.

"I'm glad you came," he finally said.

"Thank you for meeting me. I understand that you didn't have to call to warn me. I really appreciate it."

He nodded but then looked around apprehensively. Lucia glanced around, too. There were only a few other people in the restaurant. No one was paying them any attention.

"I can't be here for long. The only way I've stayed ahead of them this long is by moving around a lot. There's less chance they'll find me if I just keep crashing on a different friend's couch every night."

"They?" Lucia repeated. "Who are we talking about?"

Brent fidgeted with the strings dangling from his hood. He glanced around again. "I still not sure I want to say. Maybe it's better if you don't know. But then when I heard about what happened at your place—"

Lucia looked up sharply. "How did you find out about that?"

"I was worried after I realized someone was following me. My friend works at the police station and she told me there'd been a robbery report at your address."

"Yeah, some guy broke in. But he got away."

Brent sighed. "If it's the same people who've been following me, he'll be back."

Lucia leaned across the table. "Brent, please. If you know something, tell me. I can't protect myself if I don't know who I'm supposed to be afraid of."

His eyes met hers. "I'm pretty sure it's the Del Tinos. The crime family."

"Yes, I know who they are," Lucia whispered hollowly. She didn't even pay that close of attention to the news and she knew who they were. Racketeering, human trafficking, etc. Thus far all the government agencies had been trying to pin something on them. The Del Tinos were smart. Only Nico DelTino had seen prison time. And that was for failure to pay back child support. As far as she knew, all the Del Tinos had legitimate jobs.

But the rumors were abundant. Their family business was import/export, which just sounded shady. But every time their books were subpoenaed, even when they were subpoenaed by surprise, they came up clean. One of the big evening news programs did a story on them last year, but that was all she knew about them. She had no personal connection to them.

"Do you know them or something?" Brent asked

"No. I've never met a Del Tino, never seen a Del Tino and I have nothing in common with them other than being Italian."

Shameful

Why would the Del Tinos be coming after her? Her mind raced as she mentally sifted through all the information Noah had given her. He'd mentioned that his target was part of a drug cartel. Could that have a connection? Maybe if she could peel back the layers on what had happened that fateful day, she could finally have some real answers. Hopefully figure out a way to stay safe at the same time.

Brent leaned closer, keeping the hood of his jacket over his face. "I just wanted to warn you not to let your guard down. You have that scary guy hanging around so maybe you'll be okay. But once I gather enough cash, I'm leaving the city for good. It's harder to disappear than I thought."

"If you need anything …"

He shrugged. "Just stay safe, okay? If I could go back in time, I would have never made that call. But I didn't know you then. And they'd already paid me a lot of money. It seemed like a lot of money at the time anyway. Wasn't nearly enough for selling my soul."

"Thank you."

He nodded and then left the restaurant. Lucia waited a few minutes then followed him out. By the time she hit the sidewalk, he was nowhere in sight. She walked quickly back to the coffee shop where JJ should be in the restroom. She spied Oskar in the corner at a small table but ducked her head quickly and hustled toward the bathroom. She ran into the end stall since the middle one was occupied.

"JJ? I'm here."

"Thank God. He already opened the door once and asked if I was okay. Well, asked if *you* were okay. You know what I mean."

Lucia quickly stripped off the borrowed outfit and held it under the stall. A moment later, JJ held out Lucia's clothes. Once she was redressed, they both came out of the stalls. Lucia pulled the hat and blond wig off and JJ put them both in her bag.

"That was a lot of stress. Hopefully it was worth it?"

"Honestly, I'm not sure."

Lucia must have looked as dejected as she felt because JJ pulled her into a spontaneous hug. "Come on. Let's go get a coffee before He-man out there starts to get suspicious. Then you can tell me all about it."

Noah put his phone back in his pocket, determined not to bother Oskar with another message. When he gave an assignment, he trusted his men to do it without hovering over their shoulders. Plus, Lucia was just hanging out with a friend, nothing that Oskar couldn't handle alone.

So why was he so distracted?

Shameful

Okay truth be told, when Lucia wasn't with him, when he wasn't the one protecting her himself, it scared him. Right down to his core. Trusting someone else with her life made him edgy. But he had to remember that he'd trained these men himself. And they each cared about her. Besides, if he continued to smother her, she'd fight against that and he'd lose her. And he would rather die than let that happen. He needed to get his head back in the game and trust his team.

The comm unit in his ear crackled to life. "Boss, we've got a disturbance at the back elevator." Matthias was back at the office but monitoring the hotel security feeds remotely. It had been a real challenge to keep men available to cover all their open client cases, but luckily Matthias and his magical hacker fingers were skilled at doing the work of three people simultaneously.

"I'll go check it out."

He motioned for Dylan to stay with the client while he walked down the private hallway and swiped his keycard for the penthouse elevator. They were on a new detail today protecting a YouTube star named Sherrie Sweets who'd been receiving death threats. Noah shook his head. He wasn't even entirely sure how someone made money with online videos, but their client was the head of a makeup channel with millions of subscribers. The shit women did in the name of beauty made no sense to him, but Noah figured it didn't have to. All that had to make sense to him was the best way to protect her.

She had millions of fans, which meant millions of potential suspects that could be trying to kill her.

The elevator arrived and Noah rode down to the basement level. His team had worked in conjunction with hotel security to close off as many access points as possible. The main lobby and the back service entrance were now the only two ways to gain entrance to the hotel. The elevator doors opened to a team of caterers all wearing white uniforms. He scanned over each face, looking for anyone who looked out of place. At first glance, everything passed muster. The head of hotel security had provided a list of events taking place in the hotel that day and the catering company logo on their uniforms matched the name listed for the first event of the day.

Noah stepped aside to allow them to pass. The woman in the front smiled flirtatiously while eyeing him up and down. That's when he noticed the man in the back. Noah glanced down and noticed that his uniform didn't have the same insignia over the breast pocket as the others.

He drew his weapon. "Sir, I need for you to step aside," he said calmly. The last thing they needed was a panic.

The man looked up and then shoved the girl in front of him into Noah. She screamed and latched her arms around his neck, forcing Noah to take precious seconds to get free before he could give chase. *Fuck*.

"Matthias, I need eyes. Where is he?"

"He went down the service corridor to the laundry

room. There's a blind spot there as soon as you turn the corner. I've already alerted hotel security, and their guys are on the way."

Noah raced to the end of the hallway and paused. He should wait until the others arrived but what if there was some way out that they'd missed? This could end today, and his client could resume her life without worry that this asshole would track her down again. He raised his weapon higher and then charged around the corner.

The hallway leading into the laundry area was empty. He took a breath and then ducked into the main laundry room. It was bright and well-lit, but there was still something ominous about the huge rolling carts of sheets and the metal baskets wired to the walls holding supplies. Somewhere in the distance he heard water running.

Something shifted behind him and he swung around. "Son of a b—" Pain exploded behind his eye as something heavy banged into the side of his head. Noah backed up, waiting for his vision to clear. The shithead had gotten the jump on him.

"Ahhhhhh!" The man swung at him again and again, his movements slowing as he struggling to heave the large bottle of detergent he was using as a weapon.

Noah almost laughed at the absurdity of it all but didn't have time as one of the blows knocked him into the metal supply racks. He easily sidestepped the next attempted blow then countered with a punch to the sternum that dropped the guy to his knees.

"You must be hard of hearing. I feel like I told you to step aside," Noah growled. "Come quietly and you won't get hurt."

The asshole on his knees slanted him a glace with pure malevolence and hatred in his eyes. "I have to save Sherrie! She doesn't know what she's doing, tempting men with that harlot's paint."

Ooookay then. Noah shook his head. This dude clearly was past the point of reasoning if he thought the bubblegum cutesy makeup videos their client was known for was the devil's work. But then again, he wasn't sure why he'd bothered trying to reason with him in the first place. Reasonable people didn't stalk someone they only knew from online videos.

"Okay, well it looks like you're going to save Sherrie from prison. Come on."

He hauled the guy to his feet, grabbing him by the arm. But Noah had miscalculated. With a swift flick of a wrist, the guy had a knife out of his sleeve and was arching his opposite arm upward.

Pain, sharp and biting, slashed through Noah. He let out a low grunt as burning fire lanced his gut. He was going to kill that little shit. Just as soon as he could convince his body of mind over matter.

His breath seized in his lungs as adrenaline raced through his veins. Years of training was the only thing that saved him from serious injury as he instinctively twisted in the opposite direction. The pocketknife clattered to the floor at his feet.

Pain quickly gave way to fury. He could thank his ORUS training for that. Every operative was well versed in acknowledging the pain then deciphering it. If it was life threatening, the directive was to get to safety. If the injury wasn't life threatening, the directive was to kill the source of the pain then resume the mission. So unfortunately for this guy, he was going to complete the mission which was to protect his client.

Pissed now, Noah kicked the knife across the room and then punched the guy straight in the nose. The guy collapsed in a heap at Noah's feet.

Noah tore his shirt off and pressed the fabric against his side. The sound of footsteps had him raising his weapon until he recognized the head of hotel security.

"What happened?" His eyes fell to the guy on the ground and then on the blood-soaked shirt pressed to Noah's side. "You okay?"

"Yeah. That's what I get for trying to be reasonable." He waved away offers of help and stood back as the others dragged the guy on the floor to his feet. Suddenly all he wanted was Lucia. Visions of her danced in front of his eyes and he blinked several times to clear his vision.

"Sir, I really think you should get that looked at."

He ignored them and pushed forward into the hallway. Noah held the shirt to his side with firm pressure and focused on making it down the hallway. He had to get to Lucia.

Chapter Eleven

Noah was screwed. He knew that. He was bleeding like a goddamned stuck pig and as he eyed the road ahead of him, he was suddenly aware that walking out without medical attention may not have been the smartest idea he'd ever had.

He shook his head hard, trying to clear the gray fog threatening the edge of his vision. It wasn't as if he hadn't taken any precautions. He wasn't just running around letting himself bleed to death. He'd dressed the wound himself and he knew what the hell he was doing.

The problem was the damn dressing wouldn't hold. That's what Noah got for doing his own field dressing in the car. But now he had the added problem that all the guys were out on jobs and Lucia was at home. He could have gotten Oskar to come and help him, but that would have left Lucia unguarded. And that was never going to happen. He could have called Dylan to come for him, but he had to stay with the client.

So he was on his own.

Damn it, they were spread too thin. He knew it. They all freaking knew it. Something had to let up. But there was no way he was leaving Lucia unprotected and there was no way he was giving up on the people who counted on him. Who counted on *them*. There had to be a way. He'd have to bring on more men, or outsource, or something.

Because he couldn't keep doing this. He had been too distracted today with his attention too divided. And now he was leaking all over the place because some punk had gotten a lucky swipe. A lucky swipe that was definitely going to need stitches. He might even need a tetanus booster shot or something. That piece of shit. He'd gotten off lucky.

Shameful

If Noah hadn't evolved from the old days, he might have taken a little bit of time and some extreme pleasure in causing that little turd pain.

But you're not that guy anymore, are you? No, he wasn't. Though it scared the shit out of him when he had flashes of wanting to return to that place. All he had to do was get to Lucia. He'd he happy if he just could see her.

Truthfully, he probably shouldn't have been driving. But, short on resources and all that. He pulled into the basement garage and swiped his keycard to bypass the security gate. He pulled into his usual spot. It was concealed in the shadows, just how he liked it, but it still had easy enough access to the elevator. Just because he was stuck and bleeding didn't mean he'd ignore security procedures. He put a hand on his belly and frowned when he drew back and saw that some blood had seeped through the bandage and his dark T-shirt. Damn it. Before climbing out of the car, he placed a 911 text to the team's on-call doctor.

Maybe if he just made it into the medical bay, Lucia might not see him. *Yeah, good luck with that.* To get to the medical bay he'd have to walk straight through the kitchen. And from the kitchen, you could see everything. So one way or another, she was going to see that he was hurt. Noah sucked in a deep breath.

Now that they were trying, the last thing he wanted was for her to see him like this. He didn't want to put out a neon beacon that said, 'Hey, killer, killer. Look over here, I'm a killer.' *Yeah, some killer you are. Getting nicked by some two-bit punk. So stupid*. If his head had just been in the game, this wouldn't have happened.

Between looking for information on the Del Tinos (anything to give them leverage), trying to handle their current client caseload, and then figuring out how to stop ORUS from carrying out their contract on Lucia, he was doing too much. But was there really any other choice?

Mustering enough energy to open the door to the Range Rover, he slumped out, praying his legs would carry him at least to the elevator. It was a private elevator that went straight up to Blake Security. Once in there, all he had to do was push a button and then he could lie down. Lie down and sleep. Oh God how badly he wanted to sleep.

No. No sleeping. That was the blood loss talking. With a hand pressed over his wound, he lumbered over to the elevator, stopping once because he needed a damn break. But all he had to do was get inside the elevator dammit. Get inside, and he'd see Lucia again. That would make him feel better. He hated leaving her to go on jobs. But he couldn't let everything slide just because her life was in danger. He had to find a better solution.

It was time to bring on more men. Right now they had more work than they could handle. *Five more steps.* God, he wanted to see Lucia. She had been so twitchy this morning. He hadn't been able to get to the bottom of it. But that's what he'd been thinking about all day. That's what had him distracted. Because *she* was twitchy. Fuck, he was so pussy-whipped. He had to get a handle on that shit. *Three more steps.*

His mind, seeking a refuge from the pain, went to the one source of comfort he could conjure up. *Love*. He'd had women want to sleep with him, want to use him, want to claim him. He'd never had one want to love him before. He had no idea what to do with that. All he knew was he wasn't letting her take it back. No way. She was his now.

He still couldn't believe it. She loved him. No one had ever loved him. *Besides Rafe.* And now Lucia. Noah wanted to be in her arms. *One more step.* As soon as the doors opened, he fell in with a sigh. Almost home. Almost to Lucia. Damn he was tired. He just wanted to—

The elevator doors opened. And he forced himself to standing position. All he had to do was make it to the med bay, and then he could pass out in peace. The doctor would get here soon. They'd patch him up and he would be fine. But fuck, why was he so tired? He could barely keep his damn eyes open. But luck was on his side. There was no sign of Lucia. Because while he wanted her and her comfort, he also wanted to shield her. So it was a good thing she wasn't back yet. That was great. All he wanted to do was make it into the—

"Noah. Did you just get back?" Lucia's voice, soft and melodic, floated down like angels from heaven.

Then she appeared, her sharp eyes running over him, no doubt taking in his disheveled appearance. He hadn't taken off the bloody shirt, too much work, but had thrown his jacket over it. His fingers tightened, holding the edges of the jacket closed.

He managed to grind out, "Yeah. I'm just going to my—office." Fine. The office wasn't where he wanted to go, but it would do until the doctor got here. *Damn*. He'd been so close.

She frowned. "Noah? What's wrong? You look pale."

"I'm fine, sweetheart. I'm just gonna go to the office for a minute." He kept his back straight and forced his legs to move in the correct direction. With every step, he warned them not to shake, not to crumple. He also warned his brain that nobody was passing out. Not yet. He wasn't having any of that shit. If she saw, she'd be terrified. And she'd had enough fear to last a lifetime.

"You are not fine, Noah Blake. Look at you. Something is—" And her gaze went to the floor, and then back to the elevator and then to him. "Oh my God, you're bleeding." The horror and terror were so apparent in her gray eyes.

He frowned at her. How did she know? He was doing an excellent job of hiding this. He had protected her from himself, from the kind of life he led. She couldn't know he was bleeding.

"I'm fine." Shit, was he slurring?

The room started to spin too. Damn thing was tilting upside down. He felt drunk with the worst headache known to mankind. *It's blood loss. Stay on your feet.* If he could just keep his shit together, she wouldn't have to see him like this. He'd hoped to always protect her from this kind of shit. *How's that working out for you?*

He went down on his knees. Oh shit. The gray started to encroach on his vision, just in the periphery. It shadowed out the light, creating a pinhole effect. The last thing he registered before he went down was Lucia screaming for Matthias and Oskar.

This was it. Lucia was going to kill Noah. Okay, first she was going to make sure he was absolutely better. Then she was going to kill him.

Four damn days. Four days that Lucia had been watching Noah sleep. Four days she'd been watching the doctor change and dress his wounds. Four days he'd been going in and out of consciousness. The knife he was cut with had been rusty as hell, and he'd needed a tetanus booster.

He'd had a fever yesterday that fortunately had broken quickly. He was already getting back to himself. He grumbled at Ryan for fucking up his breakfast this morning. He was definitely feeling more like himself. She'd never been so scared in her whole damn life. Noah kept insisting it was fine.

Yeah, well he should have seen the blood. How he'd even missed the fact that he was leaking was beyond her. The slash in his abdomen was nasty. At least nothing major had been punctured. With most of the infection gone, he had less to worry about. But he wasn't out of the woods yet.

Because just as soon as he was better, she was going to kill him. How dare he try and hide something that serious from her? From what she could gather, his intention had been to go to his office, either patch himself up, kind of like he attempted to do in the car, or call Matthias to do it. He wouldn't have let her help, because even when he was hurt, he was trying to protect or shield her from himself. Who he was.

She was not down for that.

He had to get it through his thick skull that they were in this together. That he mattered to her. Her words weren't just surface words. She didn't just love the Noah who irritated her, then teased her into watching bad action movies. She loved this other side of him. The one that was edgy and dark. The one that needed her love the most.

He never wanted to show her that.

Well, too bad for him. That morning, after the doctor had left, she offered to take his dressing duties over. She knew how to apply a bandage thanks to Nonna, who'd been a nurse back in her day. She'd taught Lucia the basics.

Lucia hesitated outside his bedroom for just a moment. What if he didn't want to see her? Well tough shit for him. She loved him and he'd scared her, so she didn't bother to knock. Hell, she'd been sleeping in here every night anyway. On the couch in the corner, ready to wake up if Noah needed her. Who was she kidding? There hadn't been much sleeping happening. She'd sat in there and stared at his sleeping form. And the moment any of the guys had come in to try and relieve her, she'd threatened their balls. For some reason that made them all smile. What the hell was wrong with them? They might not fear her, but they would if they understood how much she loved him.

Her chest squeezed just thinking about how much blood he'd lost. How much worse it could have all been. That terrified her. What if she'd lost him?

So, no, there'd been no sleep for her. Not when the man she loved was in pain. Yeah, she was tired. But she was too terrified something would happen to him if she closed her eyes.

With her smile firmly in place, she pushed the door open. "Hey, I need to change your dressing."

He shifted his laptop and pinned his intense green gaze on her. "Lucia—you don't have to do that."

She ignored him. "Funny, you don't seem to know the difference between have to and want to. *And* you don't seem to understand how love works."

He sighed. "Lucia —"

She put up a hand to halt him. "No. I don't want to hear about how you are protecting me. Blah, blah, blah. The same old song and dance. We established that I love you, and you love me. That means no secrets. And after everything you've told me, I thought we were done with that. So you don't get to hide this part of yourself. The parts that need bandaging. The parts that need help. I'm just here to change the dressing so I can help you get better faster. The moment you're better again, I'm going to kill you."

His green eyes sparked with fire, and she saw that her threat to harm him had the exact opposite effect. Instead of him looking scared for his life or even remotely docile, his gaze turned predatory. "Just how do you plan to kill me? With your mouth? With that sweet tight p—?"

"Noah Blake. Stop that now." His brows popped and his eyes widened to form a mock innocent face. "I know what you're doing. You will not deflect."

"Lucia, I'm fine. You see I'm fine. And I wasn't trying to hide. I just didn't want you to do what you ended up doing; sitting by my bedside all night worrying. Freaking out."

"I will have you know that I did not freak out. I was extremely calm. I remember having to lug your injured carcass into the med room. Granted, Matthias helped with some of that. I was there and didn't become some whimpering girl, crying and screaming. I was strong. And you need to start seeing me that way. I'm not weak."

He shook his head. "I know you're not weak. That still doesn't stop me from wanting to shield you from these things. Wanting to shield you from me. I never wanted this side of me to touch you."

"Newsflash— It's already touched me. And it wasn't necessarily from you. I need to be prepared. I can't be surprised by things. I love that you want to shield me and keep me safe, but you can't have it both ways. Either I'm a child who needs protection, or a woman you see as your equal who deserves your love."

His gaze snapped to hers and held. "I'm the one who doesn't deserve your love."

Lucia shrugged. "Well, that's too bad then because you've already got it." She leaned over and kissed his shoulder. Exactly over the scar she'd given him. "Please stop hiding from me. So that we can both get started really loving each other."

"Okay, I promise you. No more hiding. From now on, you get the raw truth. Every time."

"This means, no more shielding me from things that you think would be painful. Either I'm an equal or not. If I'm not, then I probably don't need to be in your bed."

His gaze narrowed on her. Yes, she was bluffing. Because she knew well enough by now, that she would be in Noah's bed. But she needed to stand her ground. So she met his gaze directly.

Even as he worked his jaw, he nodded. "I'll tell you everything."

She nodded. "Good. Now, I need to figure out just how to get you naked without disturbing your bandage."

Noah laughed. "I swear woman, you just want me

for my body."

Chapter Twelve

Lucia brushed the hair back from his face, taking in the sharp features and the strong jaw that she loved so much. Watching him struggle to recover the past few days had been as painful as being hurt herself. The crazy man had no idea how much he meant to her, did he? Apparently not if he thought he could hide an injury or that she wouldn't want to be here taking care of him.

This was where she was meant to be.

"I definitely want you for your body. But that's not what I want the most."

At his questioning look, she pressed her hand over his heart. Lucia would never forget the gentle, awed look that passed over his face. For just a moment, Noah looked … vulnerable. She knew how hard it was for him to let her in and she'd always assumed it was because of his past. But now she was starting to think that he just had trouble believing good fortune was real. He looked at her like she was too good to be true.

So she'd just have to show him.

"I want you to hold still and let me do all the work." She gave him a stern look before pressing a gentle kiss to his bare chest.

"Yes ma'am." Noah grinned, happy to play the role of the obedient patient for now.

His eyes followed the movement of her lips as she explored the incredible chest that she never got tired of looking at. He was just so damn sexy and had muscles on top of muscles. *But even he isn't invincible*, Lucia thought as she skipped over the bandages covering his wound. She nuzzled her face into his lower belly so he wouldn't see her expression as she struggled to get her emotions under control. She'd been a basket case for the past few days and he had to be tired of seeing that. Now was the time to show him how happy she was to be with him. To make him feel good.

"And where exactly are you going, Miss Nurse?"

She laughed at his attempt to play the role. Even when she was supposed to be 'in charge' Noah had a way of taking over and directing things. It was something he did unconsciously but this time she wasn't going to allow it.

"Quiet, young man. You're supposed to be resting."

His pupils dilated slightly as she continued down his belly, following the trail of hair that led beneath the pajama pants he was wearing. She gripped the edges and tugged them down until his cock popped free. Noah let out a strangled groan when she bumped it with her nose.

"I'm resting, I am."

She gripped him firmly, tugging slightly on the soft skin, enjoying how he fit in her hand. "You seem to be recovering quite quickly. Maybe you don't need me anymore."

He shook his head frantically. "You are definitely needed here. Things have been so *hard* lately."

"Really hard, huh?"

She gripped him tighter before taking the head between her lips. She loved his slightly salty taste and the way he got even harder in her mouth. It was intoxicating to pleasure him this way and know that she held him completely within her thrall.

"Lucia, God you don't even know what it's like to watch you do that."

She glanced up to see Noah watching her, his face twisted in pleasure-pain. His eyes were fixed on where her mouth surrounded him. It normally would have made her self-conscious to have him watch, but there was no way to interpret the wild, animalistic look in his eye as anything other than pure lust.

She pulled back and licked the head, drawing a husky moan from Noah. "I like watching you, too." She deliberately kept her eyes on his as she took him deeper this time, trying to relax her throat so she wouldn't gag. The women he was used to could probably do this without any trouble, she thought bitterly. But then Lucia pushed the thought aside. He wasn't with those women. He was with her.

He only wanted her.

When he hit the back of her throat she choked a little, but it seemed to turn Noah on even more.

"You trying to take all of me, baby?" There was a warning in his voice that Lucia couldn't decipher. But her body responded to the dark eroticism in his voice, her nipples pebbling as she clenched between her thighs against a stab of desire.

He didn't wait for her answer, just circled her throat with his hand. But he must have seen something in her eyes because he cursed viciously and pulsed in her mouth.

"Lucia, I need to be inside you."

She pulled back and then climbed on top of him carefully. He'd recovered quickly over the past few days but she didn't want to take any chances of him hurting himself. He rested one hand lightly on her hip while using the other to guide his erection in place. Lucia moaned softly as she sank down on him, going slowly to give herself time to adjust. No matter how many times she was with him, she wasn't sure she'd ever get used to being filled so completely.

Noah's fingers flexed on her hip when she finally took him all the way. Lucia rocked forward slightly and then gasped at the entirely new sensation. In this position, everything was stimulated simultaneously as his pelvic bone rubbed up against her clit.

Noah's low, sexy chuckle rumbled through her. "Looks like my princess likes being on top."

She clenched around him, making him groan. "I do. You might not be able to get me off you after this."

"Well then, by all means take the reins."

He let his hands fall away and raised his eyebrows as if to say, "Game on." Lucia was more than ready to take the challenge. She rested her hands on his chest and then lifted up slightly before dropping down. They cried out together at the jolt of pleasure.

"Again," Noah ground out.

Lucia lifted her hips and then ground down on him again, crying out as her orgasm started, rolling over her in waves. She clenched around him, her hair flopping into her face as she struggled to keep the rhythm. Noah's arms came up to support her and she gladly let his hands guide her hips until she felt him stiffen beneath her.

She fell forward, careful not to rest her weight directly on him. They rested together until Noah pushed her hair back so he could see her face. She grinned at him and then kissed the tip of his nose.

"You are a very bossy patient," she muttered even as she settled into his embrace. She never wanted to leave his arms.

His soft smile made him look years younger. "Clearly I need a lot of help. You have your work cut out for you. You sure you're up for that job?"

Although the question was asked in a joking manner, Lucia understood the deeper meaning immediately. Her arms tightened around his neck.

"Just try and get rid of me."

Noah ignored the aching pain in his side as Lucia flitted around him, straightening this and plumping that. It seemed to calm her to fuss over him. The thought reminded him that she'd endured so much over the past few weeks and if their newfound relationship was going to have any chance of survival, they needed to find solid ground.

"I'm fine, Lucia. Come back to bed."

She stood next to him wringing her hands. "Are you sure? I saw that face you made when you turned over. We shouldn't have done that while you're still hurt!"

He chuckled, ignoring her chastising look. "By that, you mean climbing that sexy little body on top of me and rocking my world? We definitely should have done that. And we should definitely do it again as soon as possible." Matter of fact, if she just gave him a couple of minutes, they *could* do that again. After all, sex with the woman who loved you was really the best medicine. He wondered if he might be able to get the doc to write him a prescription for it. Would she go for that?

"Noah, be serious. I hate seeing you like this. It scares the living hell out of me."

"I've had way worse than this." And that was true. Though he wasn't going to go into any details right now. He didn't want her scared any more than she already was. She had been through enough.

Her face fell and he wanted to kick himself for reminding her just what type of man she was climbing in bed with again and again. Not that Lucia would ever forget the things he'd done—how could she—but he didn't need to remind her that he was a stone-cold killer at every opportunity either. He lived in fear that one day instead of curling into him, she'd turn away from him. No way was he hastening that moment in any way if he could help it.

A knock at the door broke the tense silence. Lucia knelt and picked up his shirt from the floor. "Just a minute." Once she'd helped him put his shirt back on and smoothed her hair, she walked over to the bedroom door and opened it a crack. "Yes?"

Matthias's voice floated through the small sliver of space. "Hey Lucia, I need to talk to Noah." When she hesitated, he continued, "You know I wouldn't bother him unless it was urgent."

With pursed lips, Lucia pulled the door open all the way and allowed Matthias to come in. Noah barely smothered a laugh at the blush working its way over her cheeks. Knowing her as well as he did he could tell what she was thinking; that the room smelled like sex, her lips were swollen and that her wild hair looked like she'd just been thoroughly fucked by her man six ways to Sunday.

It probably made him a caveman, but he grinned harder at the thought that everyone who saw her today would know what they'd been up to. Granted, everyone in here pretty much always knew what they were up to. It wasn't his fault he couldn't keep his hands off of her. She was just too damn sexy.

Besides, he wanted everyone to know that she was taken by a man who wouldn't hesitate to kill for her. She'd had enough fear in her lifetime and she deserved to know that she would be protected and cared for. He might not be white picket fence material but protection, now that he could handle.

Maybe Lucia being with a killer had its advantages.

Matthias stood next to the side of the bed. "Hey, boss. Feeling better?"

Noah shrugged. "You know how it is. I'm not dead. What more can I ask for?"

"I hear that." Matthias glanced over his shoulder at Lucia hesitantly. Although he would never say it aloud, Noah could tell that whatever he wanted to talk about probably wasn't fit for sensitive ears.

"Lucia, would you mind getting me some water? I think maybe I'm getting a little dehydrated."

She came off the wall so fast he was surprised she didn't get rug burn. She looked horrified at the idea that she might have missed something vital to his health. "Of course! I should have thought of that. I'll be right back."

"Maybe some food, too? I can come down and help you carry it." He moved to get up, knowing that she'd protest and then flopped back down when a bolt of pain lanced through his side. He'd only being playing around about needing help but apparently he wasn't as healed as he'd thought.

"Absolutely not. Stay right where you are." Lucia rushed to his side and placed another pillow behind his head. Then she aimed her glare at Matthias. "Don't let him get too riled up."

"Roger that," Matthias said with a nod. Then he waited until she left the room before he turned back to Noah. "The Feds want another meeting."

"Shit. Already?" Noah didn't have to ask why this had Matthias so freaked out. Anything that put the kid in the vicinity of law enforcement was bound to make him twitchy. With Noah laid up, that made it even more likely that Matthias would have to deal with the Feds directly since no one else was up to speed on that particular case.

"I'll be on my feet in twenty-four hours. Don't worry about it."

Matthias gave him a skeptical look. "Even if you are, do you think Lucia is going to let you get out of bed?"

Noah's brows snapped down. "Let me? The woman is no bigger than an ant. How exactly is she going to stop me?"

Matthias made a face and suddenly Noah felt like shit for indirectly pointing out the elephant in the room. Clearly Lucia had her ways of keeping him in bed. Uncomfortable silence fell between them, and Noah tried to think of anything to take their minds off the obvious.

"I'll take care of the Feds. You just keep working your magic behind the scenes. Maybe if Jonas has time, he can take over for me. He speaks that government language from his time as a cop."

Matthias gave him a mock salute but looked noticeably lighter as he left. Noah gritted his teeth and slowly sat up. He was healing pretty quickly but it wasn't fast enough for his taste. There was someone out there putting a target on Lucia's back, and he wanted to be right on the front lines tracking them down. Now with all this extra shit with the Feds, the last thing he wanted was to be confined to a sick bed.

The door swung open and Lucia appeared carrying a tray. When she saw him sitting up, she hurried to place the tray on the dresser.

"Noah, what are you doing?" She rushed to his side and placed a warm hand on the center of his back.

"Getting up. I've been in this damn bed too long."

"Well, you're going right back in this bed if I have anything to do with it. No matter what I have to do to keep you there!"

The little smile on her face told him she wasn't unaware of the dirtier implications of her words. Noah grinned.

"Well, I guess if I have no choice." He rested back against the pillows and patted his thighs. "Come on up here and keep me company, Nurse Lucia."

Chapter Thirteen

For the second time in the same number of weeks, Noah traversed the hallways of the FBI. This time, he left the kid at home. Matthias was not thrilled with the assignment. But he knew his expertise was needed, as long as Noah kept him as far away from the FBI as possible. Noah still wasn't sure this was the right thing to do. After all they had a lot going on right now. But with everything happening and ORUS still an unknown, it wouldn't hurt having an ally with government resources. If Blake Security scratched their back, they'd be forced to scratch back when he came calling.

When he was led into the Assistant Director's office, he stiffened his spine. Wincing only slightly as his knife wound pinched. Yeah, maybe he shouldn't have gone that extra round with Lucia this morning, but well, he was a bit of an addict. So what? He had gone for years without catching her. He had a lot of lost time to make up for.

Assistant Director Calhoun looked up with a smile. "Mr. Blake. Where is your associate?"

"He will not be joining us today."

The other man frowned. "That's not the job. You're not a tech expert. You can't decipher these encrypted codes. We need him here."

Once again, Noah was glad he hadn't brought Matthias. The kid was right to be twitchy about the Feds. They wanted their claws in him. And like hell was Noah going to let that happen. He hadn't helped the kid escape from one prison only to be put into another.

"We agreed to do the job. And we're doing it. I came here to give you a status update."

The Assistant Director sputtered. "B—b—but for

access to all our files, he'll need to be on site."

Noah smiled. It wasn't a particularly nice smile. It was more of a shit eating one.

"*Sir*, you want to use Matthias because he is the best hacker in the world, depending on who you ask. You think you have something here in the FBI office that he doesn't have access to?"

"But we need—"

"You need status updates. Which he'll provide through me. You don't ever need to see him in person. If he needs access to your FBI database, you can either give it to him, *or* he can take it. Let's not fool ourselves and think that he can't. So we can do things the easy way—you just give him the access, through a private server if you prefer—or he can do things the fun way. For him anyway. He'd probably enjoy breaking in more to get the information he needs. But considering you're paying us to do a job, it's probably easier if you just give it to us."

Noah didn't even flinch as Calhoun blustered and yelled something about classified information for another thirty seconds. Then when he finally realized Noah wasn't going to back down, he sat.

"If he's going to access our servers, I need one of our people at the location to make sure he doesn't access anything he's not supposed to."

"You guys are hilarious." Noah shook his head. "You think in a security firm, I'm going to let an FBI trained hacker into my systems under the guise of showing the guy what he needs? I'm not a dummy. You need Matthias. He knows not to trust you, which is why he's not here. Look, if you want our help, you'll follow our lead. Otherwise, we'll leave you to your own devices. How far was that getting you on your own again?"

Calhoun looked like he might blow a fuse. And Noah waited for that. Finally the man calmed down and sat back.

"You're never going to let us near him, are you?"

Noah shrugged. "No. But you do have access to him. You just don't have it the way that you want."

"Fine. We'll do it this way. But sooner or later, your hacker kid is going to have to answer some questions."

The hell he will. Noah forced a smile. "That's a conversation for another day. In the meantime, you want your status update or not?"

Calhoun nodded his acquiescence. And Noah gave him the information he had come to deliver. Shipping routes. Known associates. Current location of merchandise or last known port. The only thing Matthias had yet to crack was finding the head of the organization. But knowing the kid, he only needed time. When Noah was done, he sat back.

"That's all we've got for now. Matthias should have the rest of the information in a few days. Worst case scenario, a week. We'll let you know if he runs into any roadblocks or problems. But, knowing Matthias, he won't."

Calhoun sat back. "You mean to tell me, in the span of a week, he's done what my guys couldn't do in the months we have been searching for these assholes?"

Noah shrugged. "I don't know how the kid does it. I just know that he does."

Calhoun shook his head. "He could do a lot of good here. Make a difference, help people. That's not what your firm is about. Wouldn't you like to give him a chance to actually do that?"

Noah's gut twisted. Yeah, he would love to give Matthias that opportunity. The opportunity to do nothing but pure good, but the kid made his choices. And right now, it was Noah's job to protect him. At least as much as he could.

"Matthias makes his own decisions. If he doesn't want anything to do with the FBI, then I support that. Just so you know, he helps a lot of people. He just does it in his own way."

"You mean outside of the law?"

"I mean by any means necessary, and we are a legitimate security firm. You wouldn't have called us in here if you didn't think we were the good guys."

Calhoun scoffed. "Since taking on this job, I've learned to work in the gray areas. And you, Mr. Blake, you and your men are one big patch of foggy gray sky."

Noah stood. "Sometimes you need the gray before the sun comes out. I'll take my patchy, foggy sky." As he turned, a picture on John's desk caught his attention. There next to John was a man that he recognized.

He knew that face.

"Is this your family?" With a shaking hand, he picked up the frame.

The other man beamed in the self-satisfied way that only men who had it all could. He pointed to the woman. "Yes, that's my wife Diana. We've been married for almost forty years. Hard to believe!"

"And this is your son."

Calhoun puffed out his chest. "It is. He's with the Bureau as well, has been ever since he graduated."

Bile rose in Noah's throat as he set the picture down and turned to leave.

Through clenched teeth Noah murmured, "You'll get another update as soon as we have the location."

He muttered a hasty goodbye, bumping into the doorframe on the way out. The pain that ran through his shoulder and abdomen had anchored him. All his training was the only reason he got out of the building without drawing any further suspicion.

Outside on the sidewalk, he moved quickly to the second level of the parking deck to his spot. All the while, memories realigned and his mind raced over every bit of information from that day long ago. He'd never forget that assignment, of course. It had been the single worst day of his life. That case had stolen his best friend from him and changed his life forever. But now he couldn't be sure if he'd ever truly known what was going on.

That face. He knew that face. He'd studied it from every angle. Then he'd stared it down over the barrel of his gun before firing the shots that changed everything.

If his target was alive and well and not affiliated with the cartel, then what the fuck did that mean for him?

Had ORUS known they were targeting an undercover FBI agent?

Lucia tripped into the penthouse loaded down with bags. All samples for an event. She'd been closer to Noah's than to her office, and she needed to pee so bad she might burst, so she'd stopped off quickly.

She hadn't wanted to leave the ten thousand dollar dresses and accessories in the car downstairs no matter how secure it was supposed to be, so she'd had Oskar help her carry them up. She popped one of the hats on top of his head.

"You look very dashing," she said.

As she handed him the dress bags, she ran quickly to the bathroom and back to Oskar, but before they could start the trek back down, Noah came up the elevator.

She turned with a smile. "I was just going to have

Oskar help me with this. But I think that you make an even better —" When she got her first good look at him, she paused. He didn't look well. "What's wrong?"

Even Oskar, who liked to pretend he was above it all, frowned with worry. "Boss, everything okay?"

Noah swallowed hard and nodded. "Oskar, get Matthias and Jonas. I need all the information you can dig up on Assistant Director John Calhoun. And I mean everything. Even if his wife has a hobby that she writes off as legitimate business, I want to know. Anything and everything. Financial statements. Anyone with a grudge. All of it."

Oskar nodded and even though he gave Noah an ominous glare, he went to do as he was told.

Lucia grabbed ahold of his arm. "Noah? Are you okay? You look like you've seen a ghost. What happened? Are you hurt?"

He didn't say a word, just stood there, his handsome face stricken with worry. She'd never seen him like this.

Noah shook his head. And for the first time Lucia could ever remember, Noah took her hand and met her gaze, whispering, "No. I'm not okay. I think I was sent to kill an innocent man."

Lucia dropped the bags where they stood. "Come on." She dragged him through the office, into his bedroom then shut the door gently behind them. "Tell me what's going on. You're scaring me. What happened? Was it your meeting today? I thought that was at the FBI office?"

Noah shook as Lucia tugged him down onto the bed.

"Talk to me, Noah."

Noah dragged in a shuddering breath. "I don't know. I'm going over it. And I can't see. I don't know. Trying to go back further, it's all like this hazy blank space my conscience refuses to let me see."

"Tell me what you think you can't see."

He filled his lungs with air. "Okay, the day I told you about. The day Rafe died. I told you what I thought was important. How I got there. My assignment. All true. All accurate. I didn't leave anything out." He shook his head. "But I think there is something I wasn't seeing. Something I didn't know."

She rubbed her hand over the strong muscles in his back. "Okay, we'll figure it out together."

"The man I was sent to kill. I was told that he was a lieutenant for the Del Tino family."

Lucia froze. The Del Tinos. So Brent had been right to warn her about them. Her heart sank, knowing that she couldn't tell Noah about her secret meeting with Brent now. If he ever found out about that, he'd lose it. Although, she didn't have to, she reasoned. If Noah already knew about the Del Tino connection then telling him wouldn't accomplish anything.

She turned her attention back to him just in time to catch the rest of what he was saying.

"I was told that this guy was officially the second in command, but that he was the real brains behind the organization. The real reason the Feds could never get anything on them. Because the Del Tinos were clean. The old man was only a puppet figurehead. So my target that day was the lieutenant, Sanders."

She nodded. "Okay, he must have been a bad guy."

Noah rocked forward, placing his elbows on his knees. "If he was a bad guy, then why was his picture on the desk of the Assistant Director of the FBI's Cyber Division? That guy I was sent to kill is Director Calhoun's son."

Lucia frowned. "That doesn't make any sense." Then it hit her. "Oh my God, he was undercover."

Noah ran his hands through his hair in frustration. "Probably. Now I have to keep playing that day in my head. That moment I raised my gun and Rafe stood in front of it. Did he know? And if he did, how? Because we worked for the same people. Sure, Rafe was higher up than I was, but we were teamed together for a reason. Fail-safes. He would have given me that information."

"Maybe it was new information that just came in? Maybe they realized they had it wrong?"

Noah shook his head. "ORUS never had it wrong. It was their job to have it right. We were supposed to take out the worst of the worst. Not undercover FBI agents. How many innocent people have I killed? *How many?*"

His moss green eyes were anguished, terrified, and

haunted. Lucia had no idea how to help.

"Noah, if Rafe stood between that guy and a bullet, and you think he knew the guy was FBI, then that would mean he would never have let you kill any of those other people. So there has to be another explanation."

He frowned. His brows knitting tight, his brain clearly working it through. "But how did he know? He was determined to stop me, and he had never attempted to stop me before. More often than not, he acted as my spotter, my guide. What made that any different?"

"That's the real question, Noah. Why was Rafe determined to save *that* life? But yet determined that all those others had to go?"

He nodded slowly. "I need to start from the beginning. That whole day. What do you remember? From the time you woke up to the time—" His eyes shifted down to his knees. "The time that I shot Rafe. Tell me everything."

Chapter Fourteen

Lucia tucked her hands under her arms, suddenly cold. Even though she'd told Noah they'd figure it out together, what if she couldn't do it? Talking about the day Rafe had died wasn't something she knew how to do.

"I hate that I'm even asking you to do this. I'm supposed to protect you from harm, not ask you to walk straight into it."

Noah's dull voice broke through her thoughts. As soon as she saw his face it was obvious that this was taking just as great a toll on him as it was on her. He looked like he was staring straight into the pit of hell or perhaps reliving every horrible thing he'd ever done. That probably wasn't far from the truth if he was thinking about his time working for that horrible organization. She shuddered and wrapped her arms around herself trying to ward off the chill.

Lucia still couldn't believe that her brother had been a part of something like that. Then again her memories of Rafe had always been faulty, hadn't they? All she'd seen was the doting, protective, maddening big brother. That was all he'd wanted her to see, wasn't it? That's probably what hurt worst of all--that she hadn't known the brother she'd adored as well as she thought she had.

Lucia closed her eyes. *God, Rafe what were you doing?*

If someone had told her that anything could hurt worse than losing her brother, she wouldn't have believed it. But this, learning that every memory she had of their time together was faulty, was agony. It was like losing him all over again.

"You aren't asking me to do anything that I haven't tried before. I spent years in therapy trying to remember. It's just ... useless. The things I remember aren't helpful at all."

Noah looked up, his forehead pinched. "Maybe

that's not true. Because the things Rafe was doing beforehand might be the missing piece to explain this whole thing."

"Okay. I'll try. It's all such a blur sometimes."

Lucia sat on the edge of the bed next to him, her hand moving over his back in a circular motion. She wasn't entirely sure who she was trying to comfort, him or herself. Although she doubted there was any comfort to be had when trying to remember her brother's final moments.

"We'd had such a good day. It was nice weather, one of the last nice days of the fall and I'd absolutely stuffed myself on funnel cake. Rafe always thought it was funny that I loved them so much I'd eat until I was almost sick."

The emotion of remembering caught her off guard and she crumpled. Noah wrapped his arms around her and pulled her into his lap. Lucia buried her face in his shoulder and breathed in the comforting smell of Noah.

"I'm so sorry. What I wouldn't give to be able to go back and change what happened that day," he whispered.

She wiped at her cheeks. "I know. Me too. It's just hard, you know? It hits me at the weirdest times, remembering how much fun he was. He was so serious with everyone else, but with me he was a bit of a goofball. He was the best big brother."

Noah sighed. "He was an amazing big brother and he took that seriously. Which tells me there's no way he would have brought you to the site of a takedown without a very good reason. Did he say anything before you arrived? Maybe on the way there?"

Lucia shook her head. "We'd finished eating when he got a phone call. I'm not sure who it was, but suddenly he said we had to go. I kept asking what was going on but he wouldn't listen, just pulled me to the car. The whole way there he was on the phone and kept telling me that when we got there, I needed to stay hidden. I'd never seen him like that before. So I promised that I'd stay in the car no matter what."

Noah pursed his lips. "That's it? All he said was for you to stay in the car and then he left?"

"Well, actually no. He went to the trunk and he was doing something back there for a minute. I'm not sure what."

"Probably getting his weapon."

"But he gave me his gun from the glove compartment."

Noah got really quiet and Lucia realized he was trying not to point out the obvious. Rafe had been an assassin, so he would have had more than one weapon. Just another reminder that she hadn't really known her brother at all.

"Okay, so he was probably getting another gun. But that shouldn't have taken that long."

"No, it shouldn't have. Maybe he was calling someone."

Lucia shook her head. "I really don't know. I told

you. My memories are pretty useless."

Noah brushed her hair back from her face. "I'm sorry to make you relive all this. Part of me thought if we went over it something would stand out. Something that would make this whole thing make sense."

"I don't think anything is going to make sense of this."

He didn't answer but then again, she hadn't expected him to. There was no end to the shadowy paths that Noah and Rafe had traveled before his death. Suddenly Lucia was exhausted, and so incredibly furious at it all. The rage inside had nowhere to go and she practically vibrated with it. It was all so unfair that she wanted someone to blame but no matter how she went round and round in her head, it all came down to a disastrous series of events. The universe had caught them all up in an unfortunate spiral that led to death, pain and a lifetime of regret.

Each of them had been doing the best they could with the hand they'd been dealt. Noah had spent his life in service to an organization that was more evil than good, her brother had been in the wrong place at the wrong time, and Lucia had just been there to be witness to it all.

Not that any of it mattered anymore. Rafe was gone and nothing was going to bring him back. Heartbroken, all the rage left her in a rush, leaving behind an emptiness that made her incredibly tired.

"I miss him."

Noah kissed the top of her head. "Me too. And I'm sorry for dragging all this stuff up."

"I'm tired, Noah. So tired of worrying and missing him. So tired of being afraid. I just want it to be over."

"And it will be. I am going to finish it. I promise."

Something about the way he said it sent alarm skittering through her nerves. Despite her fatigue, Lucia raised her head and regarded him warily.

"What does that mean?"

But his mask was back in place, the placid expression he always wore hiding whatever she thought she'd heard. He kissed her on the top of the head gently and then lifted her, placing her on the bed. After pulling the covers over her, he stood.

"Nothing princess. Go to sleep."

Noah stared down at Lucia as she slept, peaceful at last. It had taken her a lot longer than usual to fall asleep, agitated no doubt by his questions. He hated to see her like this and it was even worse that he'd driven her to this state. It was everything he most feared about their relationship, that he'd hurt her just by nature of who he was. Even though it was unintentional, he'd hurt her today.

Never again.

He ducked into his closet and changed quickly into black jeans and a navy blue T-shirt. From a box on the top shelf, he pulled down a black skullcap to cover his hair. Considering how warm it was, too many layers would only draw attention but a hat always helped to obscure the details. Not that he expected there to be any questions about this meeting. If all went according to plan, no one would even see him arrive. However, it was ingrained in him to plan for every contingency. If he needed to be invisible, he would be invisible.

After dressing, he put in the combination for his gun safe. It wouldn't do to let down his guard around Ian, even though they'd once been friends.

He almost laughed out loud at the thought. There were no friends inside of ORUS. Men he'd worked beside, slept beside, killed beside would have taken him out without a second thought if given the order. It was the way they were trained. He wouldn't have expected anything else. When he'd gotten out, it had been a chance for a new life. A life where he could form attachments, come to rely on others for more than just back up and have something for himself. Something worth protecting.

Someone worth protecting.

Armed to the teeth, he emerged from the closet and took one last look at Lucia sleeping between his sheets. She'd twisted in the linens so they wrapped around her torso and one arm was flung up, like she was bracing herself for a blow. Even in sleep she didn't look restful anymore, and that was just one more thing that was his fault. He turned away.

"Where are you going?"

Startled, Noah looked back to see that Lucia was awake. Her eyes roamed over him, taking in the dark attire and the bulge of the weapon in his holster that even his leather jacket couldn't hide.

Without a word, she opened her arms and he was powerless to resist. He sat on the edge of the bed and leaned down into her embrace. The soft caress of her fingers against his cheek made his heart skip a beat. *God, the way she made him feel.* She didn't even know the power she held over him.

"I don't know what you're about to do and I probably don't want to know. But I don't want you to go. Stay with me." Lucia's fingers brushed over his lips like a kiss.

He inhaled, wanting to pull the smell of her scent into his lungs, maybe into his very soul. If he could carry it with him, maybe it would cover the stain of all the horrors he'd endured. Horrors that he didn't want to touch her. The thought reminded him of what he was about to do.

"I can't. Lucia, there are things that are happening. Things I can't tell you."

She squeezed his arms. "Aren't we past this? The secrets and the lies? I thought we were starting over?"

"We are but until I close out the past, it'll just keep

172

coming back to haunt us. This is something that I have to do."

"Can I come with you?"

Noah winced. Just the idea of Lucia anywhere near Ian with his cold eyes and even colder soul sent shivers through him. He didn't want any part of his past to ever touch her. She belonged in a castle surrounded by adoring knights not in the dirt with the commoners. Men like Ian, hell, men like him, didn't deserve to even breathe the same air as Lucia.

"Hell no. You aren't going anywhere. The guys are all here and this place is locked down. This is the safest place for you."

"Then that means it's the safest place for you, too. Stay with me, Noah. I don't want anything to happen to you, either."

He opened his mouth to say something, anything to dissuade her from the completely impossible idea of her coming with him but she stopped him with a kiss. It was like a drink of cool water on a hot day, her love flowing over him and healing everything that hurt. His arms tightened around her and he speared his hand into the midst of her wild curls. Lucia sighed as he peppered soft kisses over her face.

"I love you so much, Lucia. Everything I do is for you."

Her face fell, recognizing that there was nothing she

could do to change his mind. She threw herself into his arms, almost strangling him. For a moment, he allowed himself the indulgence of feeling her soft weight against him and the silk of her hair pressed against his cheek. Then he did what he knew had to be done.

Pushed her away.

"I have to go."

She turned her face away, refusing another kiss. He laughed at the petulant look on her face. Then his laugh dissolved when he saw the sheen of tears in her eyes.

"Hey, don't cry. Lucia, nothing is going to happen to me. I'm not leaving this earth before my time now that I have something to live for."

"Stupid, stupid man. Stupid, stubborn man." She muttered it angrily but all the while her fingers curled around his arm. Reluctant to let go.

"Take a bath. Watch a movie. I'll be back before you know it."

She rolled her eyes. "Don't worry your pretty little head, is that it? This is not the Middle Ages, Noah."

"I know it isn't. Because my princess has a soaker tub with jets. Unless you'd like me to call your handmaidens to bring up water and pour it in a bucket for you. I'm sure Jonas wouldn't mind."

Her lips twitched. "I'm telling Jonas you called him a 'handmaiden' just for that."

"I'm sure he won't mind. As long as I tell him he's

pretty he'll forgive me for anything."

That got a genuine laugh. He was glad he didn't have to leave her angry with him. Things had to be done; there was no getting around it. But he didn't want Lucia worrying about it.

She pulled him close and kissed him thoroughly. Just before his brain completely scrambled, she turned over and curled up with his pillow.

"Wake me up when you get home. I don't care how late it is."

"Oh I'll definitely wake you up."

By the time he got to the parking deck, he was already wishing this meeting with Ian was over. As it turned out, his princess was pretty good at negotiating. She may not have convinced him not to go but she'd made damn sure that he would hurry back.

Chapter Fifteen

The tension swirled around Noah and Lucia in the silence. What was he supposed to say? There was no answer that would work. Because at the end of the day he *was* lying to her. Had been for years. *What are you going to do when she*

finds out what you did? He couldn't worry about that now. All he could do was keep her safe. Keep her protected. That was his job after all. What he'd vowed to do. Like he hadn't been able to do for Rafe.

Lighting candles for his friend seemed like the most hypocritical thing he'd ever done. *You are not the good guy.* Despite what the padre said, God didn't hear his prayers.

"You're really going to sit there and not say a word to me?" Lucia's voice was low, but had a razor sharp edge.

He deftly navigated the Manhattan streets heading back to her apartment. "Lucia, I don't know what you want me to say. There is nothing to say. I'm doing my job. I'm keeping you safe."

She turned to him. "You see, that's the problem. I never asked for your help. I never asked you to keep me safe. I never asked for any of this. All I ever wanted was a normal life. But no, my brother was gunned down, and I had to see that. Had to *watch* that. I see it in my dreams every night. And there is nothing I can do about it, just like there was nothing I could do about it then. When you say things like you're *protecting* me, that's a joke. Because you can't protect me from the real horror." She tapped her temple. "It lives in *here*. The nightmare of my own making."

Noah's gut twisted. "I can protect you. And I will. But I need you to stop. Stop asking questions. Stop poking. Stop digging. I need you to start listening to me because shit is about to get real."

"This is not a joke. You think I don't know shit is getting real? You have your goons following me everywhere I go. My grandmother is lying to me. *You* are lying to me. When do I get my life back?"

That was one lie he couldn't tell. Because if he lied to her now, the consequences would be dire later. "I don't know."

"You see? That answer isn't good enough. Your lies are not going to cut it anymore. I'm not some kid. I'm not fifteen. You guys think I don't notice. You think I don't notice that Nonna has all that unexplained money. Seriously, you think I'm dumb enough to believe that she's been squirreling that away all this time?"

"No one thinks you're dumb."

She continued as if he hadn't spoken. "I know there are times she went without things so that I could have something. She had that cash sitting there. She could afford a better place. But she stays there. She could travel more. I know it's always been her dream to see Italy. I thought she didn't have the money. I've been working hard to give back and she's lying to me. $5000 in a tin can in the back of her cabinet for a rainy day? That is a lie. It's been nothing but rainy days for a long damn time."

"Lucia —"

"No. Don't you sit there and lie to me. I know something is going on. Noah, you had *cameras* in my apartment. That explains so much now. How you always seem to know when I'm on a date. How you always come in just in time to keep me from doing things. You realize that's sick, right? You're like some crazy big brother stalker. You're worse than my grandmother. You think I don't know that you pay half my rent?"

He whipped his head around to stare at her. "What?"

"Yes, the super stopped me last week, and he said to tell you that the owners are upping the rent next month. And of course at the time, like an idiot, I thought he assumed you were my big brother or something, since you are the one asking all the questions about security and safety, and making changes to the apartment. Now I realize it's because you pay my rent. Damn it, Noah, I'm not a child. And it's time everyone stopped treating me like one."

"I'm not treating you like a child. I'm just trying to do what's right. If Rafe were here —"

"But he's not. And he hasn't been for a long time. Any obligation you had to my brother ended a long time ago. At some point, you have to let me live my life."

"You don't understand. Damn it, your life is in danger and you don't even know how much. And instead of helping me keep you safe, you're throwing a tantrum because I pay your rent. You want to put my balls in a vice because there are things that I don't tell you?"

"Noah, this is my life. Much as you would love to live it for me, you can't. How do you know my life is in danger? What's the plan? What are you going to do about it? This is usually the point when people call, I don't know, professionals like the police. I have a right to know."

As much as he wanted to, he couldn't tell her everything. As angry as she was with him right now, she would never speak to him again. It would forever change the way she looked at him. So he did what he did best; he deflected. "You know, I find it funny how you're all over me about keeping secrets when one of the most important secrets has been held by *you*. You used my stud services, and you left out one very important detail. The secrets I keep from you aren't selfish." *Liar*. "They are *for* your benefit. Every last one of them. They're not for me. The secret you kept…you held on to it for yourself. Because you knew I would have stopped."

Lucia stared at him. "Are you being serious right now? You somehow think this compares?"

He'd relieved Ryan of duty and taken over her watch after mass. He was still just as tense as he was yesterday. She watched as his grip tightened on the steering wheel. She could always tell when a point hit too close to home. "Lucia, this isn't a comparison, but this is a conversation we *can* have. One that doesn't put your life in more danger."

When they reached her apartment, he parked the car. He and Oskar pulled their typical watch pattern, one in front, one in back. Eyes open, always aware. Oskar took his post outside her door as Noah ushered her in. The placement of his hand on her lower back made her tingle. It also made her fume.

She turned on him. "Would you get your hands off of me?"

"Would you stop being so damn touchy? I was being polite."

"Polite? Like how you walked out on me? Was that polite?"

Noah threw up his hands. "Jesus fucking Christ. You seriously are never going to understand. I woke up, ready and willing to go another round. And then I got that goddamn call. The one that told me that the woman I spent half my life protecting was in danger. So I'm sorry if I couldn't crawl back in bed for a cuddle and a poke, but I had bigger things to deal with, like keeping you safe. I had to scramble to get someone here to watch you. And then I had to get back to the office so I could comb through your life and figure out who has the means and opportunity to hurt you. And then I had to start combing through *my* past, and Rafe's past. Because you've never done anything to anybody, so why anyone would want to hurt you is beyond me. I'm sorry that I couldn't be the kind of guy who brought you breakfast in bed, but you would think I could get some fucking credit for trying to do the right thing."

"You jackass. I wasn't asking for breakfast in bed. Shit, a text would've done. Something…anything so that I didn't have to wake up alone not knowing where you were or what happened. Or wondering if that was the worst sex you'd ever had in your life. But no, you let me wake up alone with Dylan at my door." Her breath heaved out of her chest, and the flush crept up her neck as she remembered the loneliness. The embarrassment.

Noah blinked. His lips parted and his brows furrowed in confusion. "Is that what you thought? Seriously?" He shook his head. "You saw me. I could barely move. I'm pretty sure you almost killed me. I have never felt like that before."

His words didn't compute because the emotion choked all blood flow to her synapses. Before she knew it, she was spilling her guts, emotion charging every word. "You promised you would always be here for me. Do you know what that's like? When the one person you're supposed to count on is gone after something like that? You've always been my constant, and then you ran like a coward."

"I didn't run. You have to know that it was not my choice to leave you. How can you not know how I feel?"

Shameful

She felt that way? *Because you're an idiot.* Like a moron, he didn't even think to talk to her. To tell her. Give her any indication. *Instead you walked out. Shit.* Yes, he'd been reeling. He had never felt anything like that in his life. The fact that he felt that with Lucia, that shook him. He'd been her protector for so long.

Who was he kidding? She'd always been more than someone to protect. Even when she was just a kid, he'd always gravitated toward being around her. How many other twenty-year-olds had fifteen-year-old kids for friends? She was smart, and sassy, and there was something so good about her. Something that he wished would rub off on him.

Even then, he'd hoped for some kind of redemption. He was good at what he did, too good. Someone like Lucia, a part of him had hoped that being near her could save him. And she had in a way. After Rafe, he'd known he had to protect her.

"You have to know, everything I've done, I've done to protect you. And I know that you don't believe me, but it's the truth." He shoved his hands in his pockets and rocked back on his heels. He sucked at this. He didn't do feelings. Feelings got you hurt. Feelings got you killed. *Like Rafe.*

"Noah, when are you going to see I'm not fifteen anymore? I don't need protecting."

The fury and self-hatred simmered under his skin. He stormed over to her, deliberately crowding her. He needed her to see what he was. "Do you know where I come from, Lucia? The things I've done? I can't even tell you. You would be so horrified it'd change how you look at me."

She blinked up at him and shook her head. "Noah, why do you think I was a virgin at twenty-one? Why do you think that I never managed to make it work with anyone?"

She wanted answers? Fine, he'd give them to her. "Because I've been interfering. I run off anyone who even gets close to you. What's worse, I lie to myself, and I tell myself that I'm protecting you. But really, I can't stand the idea of someone else with their hands on you."

She held his gaze. "Maybe some of that was you. But if any of those guys ever had a shot, they wouldn't have been easily run off. They would've stuck. They would've stayed. Risked an ass beating. But they *all* ran. And to be truthful, they were all your stand-in. For me, it's you. It's always been you."

Noah shook his head, but he couldn't bring himself to move away from her. "I don't deserve you." *But you want her.*

"Let me decide for myself."

Noah stared down into her gray eyes. *You're not good enough for her. You are going to get her killed. She deserves better. She deserves someone good. She wants you.*

Shameful

Despite all the things that he knew about what was good for her and all the things he knew about that were dangerous for her, he couldn't stop. "Fuck it." Noah's arms snapped around her and drew her up close and he crashed his lips to hers.

Chapter Sixteen

Lucia held on to Noah's broad shoulders, trying desperately to keep pace with the kiss. Something seemed to have snapped inside of him, and the barrier that kept him so controlled was gone. His hands ran down her back and cupped her ass, kneading her soft flesh until she moaned into his mouth.

Shameful

He wasn't being gentle, and heat flashed throughout her as he took what he wanted, bending her body to his will. When he lifted her off her feet, she wrapped her legs around his waist melting into him.

"You're the only one who has ever loved me," he whispered against her neck and Lucia stilled. Was he even aware of what he'd just admitted? Afraid to ask any questions and knock him out of the moment, she squeezed him tighter, hoping she could send her love through her skin to his. For all of his faults, he'd always wanted to take care of her. It had felt like being smothered at first, but maybe it was just because he didn't know how to love. By his own words he'd never had that kind of relationship before.

But she could show him. She could be his light in the darkness, his soft place to land, and the one he opened his heart to. That was everything she'd ever dreamed.

"I do love you, Noah. So much."

At her words, he shuddered and held her tighter. She pulled back slightly so she could see his face, and if her heart hadn't already been his, it would have been right then and there. There was such naked longing and hope reflected in his dark eyes. Had any man ever looked at her like she was as vital as oxygen? Noah stared at her like some fantastical thing that he couldn't believe was real.

"I love you, Noah." She said it again because he

seemed to need to hear it.

His eyes closed and then he was kissing her again, gentler this time, like she was the most precious thing he'd ever held.

"I'm the worst man you could have fallen for, but selfish bastard that I am, I'm not turning it down. You're mine now, Lucia. Do you understand that?"

His words would have sounded ominous coming from anyone else, but everything inside of her thrilled at the idea of belonging to Noah.

"You're mine, too. And nothing will ever change the way I feel about you."

His eyes darkened then, and he pressed a gentle kiss to her throat. "I'll be better. For you, I can be better."

Suddenly, he set her gently on her feet and then unbuttoned his shirt. Lucia watched with greedy eyes as he unbuckled his belt and pushed his slacks down leaving him in just his boxer briefs. Oh wow. She'd already been with him, but she couldn't get over how big he was.

Biting her bottom lip, she bent her arm under and pulled down the zipper of her dress, shimmying her hips until it pooled at her feet. Underneath she wore a plain black bra and panties, nothing special, but the way Noah sucked in his breath at the sight made her feel like a goddess.

"Make love to me, Noah. Just us, no secrets, no

Shameful

lies."

He knelt and picked her up, holding her against his chest as he strode down the hallway to her room. Lucia giggled when he dropped her on the bed, spreading her arms to keep from bouncing all over the place. Noah smiled and then crawled over the bedspread toward her.

"I love that sound. All I ever want is to see you this happy, Lucia."

She ran a finger down his muscular chest and then circled his erection with her palm gently. His lashes drifted down on a strangled groan, and then he shot her a look that told her his erotic retribution would be swift.

"You have everything you need to keep me happy."

She stroked him gently and he groaned. "Fuck, princess, that feels so good."

Feeling bold, she slid her hand down his boxers and Noah cursed low even as his erection twitched in her hand. His hips pushed into her hand and he squeezed his eyes shut as he bit his bottom lip. She liked this kind of power. Liked how it felt to make him lose control.

When her fingertip found the bead of liquid and spread it over the tip of his erection, he shuddered but then quickly stilled her hands. "Princess, you have to stop. My control is already thin."

She frowned. "But I was exploring."

"I promise you, you can explore later. Right now, I want my mouth all over you."

He settled between her legs, his hard length rubbing against her panties in a way that made her shiver. His lips danced over her collarbone and then brushed over the stiff peaks of her nipples. She arched her back as the tingle of electricity shot straight to her core. While he wrapped his lips around her nipple and tugged, his other hand teased her free nipple, drawing it into a tight bud.

Lucia arched and bucked into each caress even as Noah whispered against her flesh. "You taste so good, princess." He slid his hand down over her ribs, to her hips, then to the juncture of her thighs. When his fingers moved the cotton to the side, she arched up trying to pull his fingers inside where she wanted them. Noah was happy to oblige, thrusting two fingers deep.

With a strangled curse, he pulled back long enough to yank her panties down her legs. Lucia sat up slightly, struggling to unhook her bra. There was nothing she wanted more than to feel his skin against hers. Noah reached behind her to assist and then threw the bra over his shoulder.

He looked down to where her legs had fallen open and his lips curled up briefly before he slid down and kissed the top of her mound. His tongue found her clit at the same time as his fingers found their way back home. Lucia moaned, and her head fell back at the dual sensations of being licked and penetrated.

"Always so wet for me," Noah murmured appreciatively.

Lucia didn't have time to be mortified by the comment because he added his thumb to the equation, circling and rubbing until all the energy in her body shattered into a million fragments of light and heat. He stayed with her as she bucked beneath him, his tongue lashing over and over, drawing every bit of sensation from her.

"Noah, please!"

All she could do was cling to his shoulders as waves of pleasure rolled through her, spreading from the top of her head down to the very tips of her toes. When she could finally open her eyes again, Noah was watching her with a look of dark satisfaction.

"Look at me, princess. I want to see your eyes."

As soon as their eyes met again, he climbed up her body and arranged her legs over his shoulders. Lucia gulped in air, trying to ready herself for him to take what he wanted. When Noah made love, he didn't hold anything back and she was so ready for it. He didn't seem to think that she could handle his deepest secrets, but she knew that no one else could ever accept him the way she could.

His hands settled on either side of her face. "I love you, Lucia."

She gasped at hearing those words for the first time and then again when he thrust deep. The position allowed her no room to hide and she felt tears well in the back of her eyes. Not from pain but from the stark intimacy of taking him this way, looking deeply in his eyes, accepting everything he had to give.

"I love you. I love you. I love you." He whispered it over and over as he took her hard, like he was afraid that if he didn't say it enough that it wasn't real.

But that had been Noah's only exposure to love, hadn't it? Something that didn't last, something that could be taken away from you at any moment. Tenderness swelled inside for this gentle giant of a man who was so afraid to love but had so much of it to give. Lucia's orgasm broke and she sobbed against his shoulder at the intensity of it.

Noah stilled and she felt him shuddering as his own pleasure took over. She wrapped her arms around him, never wanting to let go of what they'd found together.

For years, Lucia had dreamed about this, making love to him with no reservations. Now it was here and she could hardly believe this was her life. That she could touch him, kiss him, and hold him whenever she wanted, seemed too good to be true. But maybe the universe was done torturing her and she was finally going to get her happy ending.

Shameful

A shot rang out.

Lucia moaned and tossed her head back and forth. She didn't want to see what happened next. For the first time, she was aware that she was dreaming but could do nothing to stop the horrible images from unfolding before her. Lucia sobbed silently as she watched Rafe rummage through the glove compartment of his car, knowing what was coming next.

"Stay here. No matter what, okay?"

In her dream, Lucia smiled. She remembered thinking that her brother was always so worried about everything and that he really needed to learn to relax.

"Okay, fine. But really, where am I going to go?"

"I'm serious, Lulu."

Rafe pressed a gun into her palm and Lucia gasped. She'd never held a gun before, and the cold metal seemed so heavy in her hand.

"Take this. If something happens... you drive out of here as fast as you can."

"Rafe, I can't drive yet."

"I've taught you enough. Just drive, Lu. As fast as you can."

A shot rang out.

Lucia tossed her head and whimpered.

"Rafe!"

She wanted to protect him, to hold him close but where his body was supposed to be, there was nothing but blood. It flowed around her in rivers that threatened to sweep her away. She raised the gun and fired.

"I love you. Come back," she sobbed, looking around desperately for her brother's body but it was too late. He was gone.

A shot rang out.

Suddenly, she saw the events happen with crystal clear precision, something that had never happened before. The man who'd shot her brother stood right in front of her, and she could see his profile clearly. Tall, dark hair, and so handsome. She'd come to love him over the past few years as much as she loved Rafe. Suddenly, his face morphed from a blur into Noah's face.

Lucia trembled in her dream, watching as the shot rang out and Noah jerked. She'd shot him. The shock of it was so horrifying that she woke up with a scream on her lips.

She turned her face into her pillow and sucked in a desperate breath. Noah slept next to her unaware, and she calmed herself by concentrating on the idea that dreams were just her mind's way of coping with the tragedy. It was just so strange for her mind to torment her by replacing the things she couldn't remember with

Noah's face. Was it because of the recent changes in their relationship? Was she feeling guilty for moving on with Noah instead of searching for her brother's killer?

The explanation actually made sense and helped to slow her racing heart. Maybe it was time to listen to Nonna for once and go back to the therapist she'd seen right after Rafe's death. If she was ever going to move on and live her life, she had to come to terms with things. It wasn't abandoning her brother to want a normal relationship with a man who loved her. She was finally on the verge of getting everything she'd ever wanted, and she didn't want to let her fear hold her back.

Noah shifted slightly, and she could tell when he woke up because he stiffened, probably unused to having someone in bed with him. He'd confessed once, after she'd teased him about being a ladies man, that he'd never shared a bed overnight with anyone.

"What's wrong?" he whispered.

"Nothing. Just a bad dream. Sorry I woke you."

"Come here, princess." He held out his arm.

Determined to move past the horror of the nightmare, she curled up against him, resting her head on his chest. The solid beat of his heart lulled her until she could breathe easily again.

"Better?"

"Yeah. I'm glad you're here, Noah." She knew he didn't relax easily and knew what a big deal it was for him to spend the night with her.

"I'll always be here for you, Lucia. No matter what."

THE SOUND OF gravel crunching under the weight of his tires was the only company Noah had as he drove past the warehouses that lined the Hudson River.

Yeah, the meet was cliché, but he knew the spot. Had multiple exits just in case something went wrong, just in case. He wasn't taking any chances. There had been a point long ago when he would've trusted Ian with his life. The problem now was that he didn't trust *anyone* except his own men and Lucia.

Ian was already there when he arrived, and that fact made Noah chuckle, as it had been *his* intention to be early. It also made him twitchy, as he had no idea how long Ian had been here. His old friend could've scoped out places to attack.

So much for old friendships.

When Noah exited the car, Ian smirked at him as he lounged back against the Audi sports car he drove. "I see you like to come early."

Noah shrugged. "Well, since you're already here, that makes me late."

Ian chuckled. "Good to see you, kid."

He smiled hearing the term. How long had it been since he'd heard that? It shouldn't be a surprise. Ian had always called him a kid. But he had lived ten lifetimes since then.

"I'm hardly the kid anymore, right?"

Ian only inclined his head. Ian hadn't been much older than Noah was now when Noah had first joined ORUS. And he'd been in for at least a decade before Noah had ever shown up.

"That's true." Ian pushed himself to standing with crossed arms. "So you wanted to talk. Talk."

Noah his gaze straight on. "You have answers I want."

"And you know I can't give you much."

Noah rolled his shoulders. "So, us working side-by-side doesn't count for anything? Me saving your life doesn't count for anything?"

A muscle in Ian's jaw ticked. "It counts for enough. I called to warn you. You should've gotten the girl the fuck out of town. New cover. New identity. You should've put her on the run. But instead you kept her around. Not my fault if someone comes knocking on your door because of it."

"Trust me, if I could have I would've handed her a passport and sent her on her way. But this is Rafe's little sister. No way was she going to run and I couldn't leave her unprotected. If I had tried that, she would've found her way back. Besides, didn't you train me to take care of the threats and not spend my life watching my back?" He stared at his former friend. "You regret teaching me that now, right?"

"You weren't supposed to use it to get the fuck up

out of the organization," Ian said, the hint of emotion in his voice surprising Noah.

Noah shrugged. "I did what I had to do. And I found a way to get it done. Sorry if that blindsided you but I couldn't stay. I'm glad I didn't. Considering what I know now."

Ian tossed up his hands. "Come on, kid, were you really that naïve? We are assassins. We kill people. How did that fact escape you? Sometimes you don't like the name that's called up. But that's the job. You do the recon, you take out the target. Unseen, undetected, and you live to fight another day."

"Except this time, the target is the woman I love."

Ian flinched. "You went and fell in love with her? Man, oh man, you are the dumbest smart dude I know. You know how risky it is to partner up. To care about someone. To attempt to have a family and shit. That is a disaster. It gives enemies the chance to hurt you."

"Look, it wasn't the plan. For years I've been protecting her. She's Rafe's sister. I was doing right by her. Then things changed. What was I supposed to do? Stand by and let you kill her?"

Ian shrugged and shook his head. "I told you, I didn't take the job. But someone else did."

Noah inclined his head. "Who is it? I recognized the moves in her apartment when I fought the guy. He wasn't big enough to be you. Tall, but not over my height. Nasty son of a bitch, too. I have the bruise on my thigh to prove it.

But he tried like hell not to kill me, so it must not be one of your new guys."

Ian frowned. "What are you talking about? No one was sent yet. Roland, one of our newer guys, just took the job. Most of the rest of us were feeling too nostalgic to pick off Rafe's sister."

Noah shook his head. "Happened a little over a week ago. After we talked. Some guy broke into her apartment, had a tussle. The guy was a pro. Good. He got some shots in and I got some hits. It was a draw. You know if it was anyone else other than ORUS, it wouldn't have been a draw."

"You're telling me, some fool got the jump on you? You're out of practice, my man." The thought seemed to amuse Ian.

"No. I'm not. *He was that good*. Never seen anyone like that. You got any new guys that are fast? Like you used to be?" He hid his smile at Ian's reaction to the dig. Nothing like hearing about how fast you 'used' to be. They were badasses, but they had their egos just like everyone.

Ian put out a hand. "No man. I already told you. Roland just took the job. Today, in fact. He's going to make an attempt soon, very likely tonight. I assume you have your guys on her. The kid is eager to please, so I hope you make his life difficult. Never did like that kid if I'm being honest. We didn't send anyone to you before."

Noah's whole fucking world turned upside down.

One, somebody was coming for Lucia. Two, ORUS hadn't sent someone before. That meant all kinds of crazy shit, and he was in no mood to deal with that yet. Right now, he had to see Lucia.

"You're sure he'll try tonight?"

"I would. So probably. I thought you'd be smart and get the fuck out of town. Not sit there playing house with ORUS agents about to crawl up your ass."

Oh shit. He'd left her alone. Not alone, the guys were there. All of them. And the penthouse was a fortress. Thank fuck, but he should be there. Protecting her. He spun and hopped back in his Range Rover, gunning the engine.

Right now one thing really scared him. If ORUS was only coming after her today, then why was the other player trying to kill her? Why the fuck did he want Lucia? Trouble was coming and he had to get to her.

"Okay, one of you needs to explain the timeline of these movies to me. So did the series reboot and they just went back in time to show progression? Or is this a brand-new timeline because they sent Logan back to stop Mystique and Tyrion Lannister. Now they can do whatever the hell they want? I'm confused."

From the opposite couch and the massive lounge area, Oskar groaned and rolled his eyes before hitting pause on the DVD player.

"Jonas, please explain to her again how the X-Men movies work. Because if I have to try and explain the back-in-time thing, and the Logan thing, and the Phoenix thing, my head is gonna explode."

Next to her, Jonas chuckled. "Lucia, you know you're driving him insane, right? He loves all things X-men."

She bit back a laugh. "Yes, I know. But I'm just trying to figure out how everything works together. And then what does this mean for the whole Marvel universe? The whole Avengers situation and Jessica Jones, Daredevil, and Luke Cage? Because I'm confused. It's like they don't even know about each other, but they sort of do."

She gave Oskar her best wide-eyed innocent look. The dude looked like he was gonna pop that vein on his forehead.

"Lucia," Jonas warned, "You keep this up and he will eat all the chocolate in this house just to spite you."

She narrowed her gaze on Oskar. "You wouldn't."

The big German nodded and gave her an evil smile. "You better believe it sweetheart."

Lucia could only blink. Jesus. He was gorgeous enough when he was all stoic and stern. But when he smiled … Jesus H. Christ. He should do that more. Not that he in any way compared to Noah. Though, she was probably biased. She squared her shoulders and called his bluff.

"And then the guy that's like super fast on the X-Men, isn't that the exact same character who was one of the twins who died in Sokovia?"

She knew she was driving Oskar crazy. For someone who was so buttoned up, whenever he was watching one of these movies, he became a total comic book geek.

He threw himself back on the couch and cursed under his breath in German. His accent was almost unintelligible most of the time unless he was irritated like now.

She giggled. "So, you're not going to hold my chocolate hostage?"

"You and I both know that would make you a raving lunatic who would make Noah pay. Then Noah would make all of us pay," he grumbled.

On the other couch, Matthias said nothing. The two of them still hadn't gotten back on an even keel. When he headed to the kitchen for popcorn, she waved at Oskar to turn the movie back on and followed him.

"Hey, Matthias?"

He didn't turn as he pulled a beer from the fridge. "What do you need?" His voice was arctic. Not a hint of warmth.

Okay, so he wasn't going to make this easy. "Can we talk?"

Now he did turn. Gone was the affable, always smiling Matthias. This guy was harder. Sure, she'd seen him smile since that day at the fashion show. But it was as though those smiles never reached his eyes.

"We don't need to talk. We're cool." He moved to brush past her, and Lucia reached for his arm. He immediately flinched away, and she held her hands up.

"I'm sorry. I just thought—we were friends. And then everything changed. I know, I didn't say it that day. I was way too freaked out. But thank you. What you did. I don't know where I'd be or if I'd even still be alive."

He shook his head. "I was doing my job, Lucia. That's the end of that."

"Yes. You were. And I'm sorry if I've been distant. We were friends before that day. And we've both sort of tried to pretend like everything is fine. But I saw a part of you that I have never seen before, and I have to tell you it scared me. Then you shut down. I'm trying to figure out how we get back to being friends again."

He sucked in a deep breath and then set his beer on the counter. "It's fine, Lucia. It's because I care about you that I dug into the part of myself I never look at. I'm not that guy. That sweet funny guy. I'm this guy. Cold, calculating. A killer. That other guy was a mask I used to put on like a suit every day. I don't have to do that now. The job was to look after you. There was no way in hell anyone was going to hurt you on my watch. Even if it meant letting out a part of me that's hard to shut back in the bottle."

She studied him closely. "I'm sorry you had to dig into that part of yourself for me. Sorry any of you—" Before she could even get the thought out, his arms wound around her like a vice and he dragged her to the ground. Something ricocheted off of the granite countertop, sending shards everywhere.

From the living room, Jonas and Oskar cursed and there were more loud pops of gunfire.

Matthias reached above him and grabbed a gun that was stored underneath the countertop, pulling her with him to the other side of the island. Shots rang around them and all Lucia could do was curl herself into a ball.

Matthias tucked her firmly in front of him where the bullets wouldn't hit her, and he stood firing off two rounds. The loud *bang bang pop pop* sounds echoed in her ears.

From the other room, Jonas shouted, "*Motherfucker*. Oskar!"

Then there was silence. Wait, not entirely silent. She kept hearing the *pffft, pfft* sound, but couldn't identify it.

Usually the sound was quickly followed by what sounded like things breaking or being hit, or shattering. And then she heard the real gunshots, their booming noise echoing all around her in the penthouse.

There was a moment of silence then she heard a whistle. Somewhere to the left of the kitchen. Two short whistles, then Matthias whistled back.

When he turned his attention to her, he whispered,

Shameful

"Listen, we're going to get you to the panic room okay? I need you to do exactly what I tell you. I'm trying to keep you safe."

Lucia nodded then took the hand that he proffered. And then they were running. Her feet were bare, and the shards of glass and marble shredded her soles but she didn't even stop to think. But they didn't make it far.

Suddenly there was a loud *oomph*, and Matthias was flying forward. She was forced to let go of his hand, and she stumbled backward on her hands and feet. Gunfire rained around her, and all she could do was duck and tuck her head.

In front of her they were fighting; Matthias, Jonas, Oskar. All of them fought a man in all black, complete with black mask. But Oskar only seemed to be able to use one arm. She watched in horror as the man in black grabbed Oskar by the hair then aggressively assisted him to the ground ... headfirst. The resounding crack made her stomach lurch.

Fear and anguish took hold of her frontal cortex. All this was for her. *They're all going to get hurt.* She had to do something.

Anything.

Matthias and Jonas traded shots with the guy. Somehow Matthias was better at blocking the blows and Jonas took a hard kick to the head.

Lucia wanted to scream, "Leave Matthias alone.

Take me. Do whatever it was that you want with me." But she sat frozen. She didn't want to see Matthias hurt.

But Matthias wasn't getting hurt. He was on his feet and going hand-to-hand with the guy. Trading punches and elbows and kicks in a flurry of moving arms and legs. And then she saw it. This wasn't her friend Matthias. He wasn't affable and lovable. That was his Matthias suit like he'd said. Matthias, like Noah, was a killer.

She'd seen a hint of it at the fashion show. But this … this was the real him. The guy procured a knife, and instead of showing fear, she was pretty sure Matthias smiled. It wasn't a nice smile. It was a smile that said he was going to enjoy killing him.

Behind them, Jonas shoved himself to standing and went after the guy, then it was two-on-one again. Jonas and Matthias, bearing down on the guy. Backing him off.

The guy in black reached into his pocket, pulled something out, and threw it straight into Jonas's face. The next thing she knew, Jonas was wheezing and coughing, clutching at his throat. Lucia ran over, trying help. Trying to do something. But her movements must've alerted the attacker to her position because his attention drifted to her for just a split-econd.

Just long enough for Matthias to get a good hit. The attacker's head snapped to the side, and Matthias kept hitting him. His handsome features a mask of rage and … joy. He was enjoying himself. The man in black started to go down.

Shameful

She tried to grab Jonas by the shoulders and drag him back into the kitchen. To get something that could wash whatever it was that was hurting him off his face.

Matthias was going for the guy, sitting over him. *Pop. Pop*. He got him twice before the assailant managed to deflect one of the punches. In a split second they rolled and fought over the knife.

Shit. Oh shit. Oh shit. Matthias was going to die. They all were. Because of her. No way was she letting that happen. She searched for a weapon. *Anything*.

And then she noted the recycling that hadn't been taken out. There were some wine bottles in there. She left Jonas where he was and ran into the kitchen, well aware now of the cuts she was getting on the bottom of her feet.

Her first stop was one of the towels. She wet it and then snagged one of the wine bottles out of the recycling bin. Running back to Jonas, she wiped his face. And he was able to blink up at her. At least that was something. What the hell was he mouthing? Oh. Run. He was saying run. Her gaze slid to the door. And flickered back at her friends. Oskar was down, unconscious. Jonas was also incapacitated. And Matthias, if she didn't do something, he'd die. Hell no. She wasn't leaving her friends.

She wiped Jonas's face and shook her head. "I'm not running."

And then she went straight for Matthias and the asshole in black. As they tumbled and fought for the knife, she raised the wine bottle. Matthias shook his head. She ignored him, trying to bring the bottle cracking down on the guy's head, but it was as if he sensed the movement and deftly rolled out of the way. Putting him on top of Matthias and giving him the leverage with the knife. Hell no.

She ran right up to him and wrapped an arm around his neck, trying to drag him off Matthias. And then she remembered all the things that Noah had taught her. *Eyes, nose, throat*. She tightened her arm around his trachea. But she didn't have enough strength to pull him off Matthias. Switching tactics, she took her thumbs and pushed them straight to the guy's eyeballs and he howled, but he didn't let go of Matthias.

Instead, he delivered a straight shot to Matthias's nose. She could hear Matthias's head ricochet off the wood floor before he groaned. He reached out for the guy, but the other guy just shoved at his chest and stood, then he came straight for her. She scrambled for her wine bottle again, raising it like a weapon. All he did was shrug his shoulders, rolling them back. Preparing for her assault.

Jonas pushed himself to standing as he blinked rapidly. He held his hands out in front of himself. He couldn't see. *Shit*. Now was a good time to run. Spinning around, she bolted, her bare feet crunching on the glass and the shards of marble. She just needed to get to the stairs or in one of the halls and scream bloody murder. Someone would come to help her. To die? What if this guy had brought friends?

She could hear his heavy footfalls behind her. And then the blood on her feet must have made her slip because next thing she knew she was ass over teakettle, and she had barely made it around the foyer.

But she didn't hit the ground with a crack. Instead he lifted her and threw her over his shoulder. As he positioned her, he wrapped something around her waist, like a belt. She used the wine bottle to hit him in the kidneys. She kicked. No way in hell she'd go quietly. But his grip was too tight.

"Relax, Lulu. You only hurt yourself doing this." He was carrying her back toward the spare bedrooms.

Oh fuck no. No way in hell.

They passed Jonas who was now back on his knees as he blindly tried to get to Matthias. Matthias was also getting back up. But Oskar didn't move. *Fuck*. She fought as hard as she could.

Because no one was coming for her. Noah was out looking for answers. He wouldn't be back for God knows how long. She couldn't let him take her in there.

"Lulu, I told you to stop it."

And then it filtered in. That voice. The way he said her name. *Oh my God*.

"Rafe?"

His hands stilled. But he didn't say anything. Nor did he remove his mask.

Her voice was hoarse, and she asked again, "Rafe?"

The crack of gunfire fire hit the doorjamb just as they passed through it. The guy tossed her to the bed and looked around, and then Lucia saw him pull a knife and throw it toward the door. All she heard was a grunt of pain and then another crack of gunfire. The guy looked from her, to the door, then back to her again, cursed, and went for the window. He took something from his hip and attached it to the edge of the windowsill. Then he hopped up and was out the window.

Coughing, the shock still flooding her body, she stumbled to the window. They were in the freaking penthouse, where was he going to go? Then she saw what was on the windowsill. A grappling hook. He rappelled down the building to the wide balcony several floors down then he dashed inside.

Oh God. That voice. Could it be? Behind her, she heard the one voice that could break through her terror and her anguish and her … hope.

"Lucia. Oh my God. You're okay?"

She turned to find Noah in the doorway. He stumbled and reached for her as though she were his lifeline. She limped and met him halfway. He snapped his arms around her and let the cocoon of his warmth calm her as she sank into him.

"Where is he? Did he hurt you?"

All she could do was shake her head and point to the window and the grappling hook still attached to the sill. "He went out the window." It was on the tip of her tongue to tell Noah that she thought it was Rafe. But she knew how that would sound. Her brother was gone.

So then who the hell was it that just used her nickname?

THANK YOU for reading *Shameful*, the second book of the exciting new romantic misadventure trilogy, *Shameless*. The Shameless Trilogy continues with *Unashamed*.

New York Times & USA TODAY Bestselling Author
M. MALONE
USA TODAY Bestselling Author
NANA MALONE

He is the thing that goes bump in the night. He is a liar, a protector...a killer... He is Noah Blake.

...And I love him.

Everything I thought I knew about the night that changed our lives has been turned upside down. I have no idea who to trust, but the one thing I do know is that I am his...And I will do anything to protect him.

EXCERPT of *Unashamed*
© June 2017 M. Malone and Nana Malone

As Noah Blake surveyed the remnants of his destroyed office, his mind blocked out everything but the task at hand. He couldn't think about the fact that Matthias had been beaten almost to a pulp. He had to temporarily forget about Oskar's dislocated shoulder and that Jonas had been gassed and could possibly lose his sight.

He definitely couldn't remember the image of Lucia sobbing on the bed after almost being kidnapped or the fact that if he'd been sixty seconds later, she'd have been lost to him. Noah tensed and pushed the mental image into a closet and locked the door.

Not going there.

"Jonas, keep rinsing your eyes. The doctor is on his way."

His friend gave him a thumbs up and splashed more water in his eyes as he stood over the sink in the kitchen. Oskar sat at the counter, resting his arm on the surface while holding an ice pack to his shoulder. He'd probably be back to normal before any of the others. Noah had already popped the arm back in socket but it would be sore as hell for a few days. The doctor was going to give him hell for doing it himself, but Oskar had been suffering and they'd all had something dislocated at some point. He wasn't going to leave his friend in agony when he could fix the problem.

Too bad he couldn't do something to help the others. He hated feeling so helpless.

Noah knelt next to where Matthias was stretched out on the floor and placed another ice pack against his jaw. His face had already swollen beyond belief, the eyelids so puffy his face was unrecognizable. It was a miracle the kid was still conscious. Noah suspected it was pure force of will because Matthias would hate the idea of being unconscious and at the mercy of others.

"I wish you weren't so fucking stubborn, kid. You need to be in the hospital."

"No way. Not putting you at risk."

His words were muffled and slurred, but Noah could easily understand him. Mainly because he'd known what Matthias would say even before he spoke. With how paranoid the kid was about his information being in the system, he'd have to be literally kissing the Grim Reaper before he'd consent to being hospitalized. Looking at his swollen, distorted features, Noah honestly thought he wasn't too far from that scenario. He looked bad. *Really* bad.

"Fuck putting us at risk. This is your life, Matthias. We can find a way to keep the heat off of us. We'll say you were mugged or something. Shit."

"No hospital. Please."

It was the please that did him in. He could feel the waves of panic coming off the other man. Nothing short of knocking him out completely would get Matthias through the doors of a hospital, and Noah didn't have the heart to put him through any more traumas.

"Doctor is here."

He looked up with relief at the sound of Ryan's voice. The only stroke of luck so far had been that Dylan and Ryan hadn't been in the office when they'd been hit so they were available to help out. Well, maybe it wasn't luck. The asshole who'd taken out half his team had probably known damn well exactly how many people were in the building. He seemed to have planned it all out. The only thing he hadn't counted on was Lucia.

Noah glanced over to the couch where she'd been sitting for the past ten minutes. She'd been inconsolable at first, clinging to him with all her strength, but now she was disturbingly silent. He'd tried to talk to her but was met with a blank stare each time. He wasn't sure if she was going into shock but in the midst of all the other physical injuries, he'd had no choice but to just keep her in his eyesight while he tried to take care of everyone else.

Jonas had told him that she'd refused to run. It enraged him that she'd put her life in danger, but he couldn't deny that he was also proud as hell that she was so courageous. Not that he wasn't going to paddle her ass later for that stunt.

"Where should I start?" Dr. Breckner's eyes flared slightly when he took in Matthias's appearance. He moved forward without waiting for an answer.

Noah stood back so the doctor could examine him. The doctor had been their on-call physician for years, but they'd never had to call him for anything this severe. It was usually stab wounds, cracked ribs, or the rare graze of a bullet. Matthias looked like he was sporting all of the above and then some.

A young woman, probably only a little older than Lucia, approached her. "Hi, my name is Robin. I'm a nurse with Dr. Breckner. Are you injured?"

Lucia shook her head. The nurse glanced over at Noah uncertainly. He really wanted to argue, but something about the set of Lucia's mouth made him rethink trying to force her just then. Noah motioned for Robin to assist Jonas.

"Jonas, there's a nurse here to take a look at your eyes."

His friend blinked rapidly but gave a thumbs up to show that he'd heard. Apparently he still couldn't see anything. *Fuck.* The nurse approached, speaking in low tones. Satisfied that the medical professionals had things in hand, Noah approached the couch where Lucia sat staring at the wall.

"Lucia, you really should let the doctor examine you."

She didn't move or acknowledge his words in any way. Noah put his arm around her shoulders and she flinched. His heart sank. God, she looked so small and vulnerable sitting here all alone, but it looked like she didn't want his comfort. Not that he blamed her. If he hadn't been so damned insistent on going to see Ian tonight then he would have been here to protect her. It was the same thing over and over again.

He just kept letting her down.

Then his mind flashed to Lucia curled up on the bed sobbing her heart out and his blood chilled for a totally new reason. He had no idea what that bastard had done to her before he'd gotten there. Had he ... touched her? She was showing some of the signs of sexual assault, especially not wanting to be touched.

Dylan waved at him, trying to get his attention. Noah thrust his hands through his hair roughly, taking out his frustration on the strands. The pain centered him, bringing him back to the present. He had a team of people counting on him to get them through the storm and to safety. A team that included Lucia. Their safety was paramount so he had to get his head out of his ass.

"I'll be right back, princess." He murmured the words to her without expecting a response so he was shocked as hell when she nodded.

"Please tell me you have some good news," he growled as he approached Dylan.

The other man blew out a breath. "I found a place that's big enough. It's not exactly up to our usual standards but maybe that's a good thing in this case. It's underground."

Noah looked around at the marvel of glass and steel that had been his pride and joy and a symbol of everything he'd overcome. In the end, it had been a weakness because of all the glass and how open it was. When they rebuilt, he was going for bulletproof glass for sure. In the meantime, going underground was perfect. It wasn't going to look like much but it would be a rock solid hideout while his team recovered and he spent some time in the trenches to smoke out the bastard targeting them.

Lucia. Targeting Lucia. Because he couldn't forget for one moment what this was really about.

"Then underground we go."

** *Unashamed* is available now!

Shameless

New York Times & USA TODAY Bestselling Author
M. MALONE
USA TODAY Bestselling Author
NANA MALONE

New York Times & USA TODAY Bestselling Author
M. MALONE
USA TODAY Bestselling Author
NANA MALONE

New York Times & USA TODAY Bestselling Author
M. MALONE
USA TODAY Bestselling Author
NANA MALONE

ABOUT THE AUTHORS

New York Times & USA TODAY Bestselling author **M. MALONE** lives in the Washington, D.C. metro area with her three favorite guys: her husband and their two sons. She holds a Master's degree in Business from a prestigious college that would no doubt be scandalized at how she's using her expensive education. j

Independently published, she has sold more than 1/2 million ebooks in her two series THE ALEXANDERS and BLUE-COLLAR BILLIONAIRES. Since starting her indie journey in 2011 with the runaway bestselling novella "Teasing Trent", her work has appeared on the New York Times and USA Today bestseller lists more than a dozen times.

She's now a full-time writer and spends 99.8% of her time in her pajamas.

minxmalone.com

USA Today Bestselling Author, **NANA MALONE**'s love of all things romance and adventure started with a tattered romantic suspense she borrowed from her cousin on a sultry summer afternoon in Ghana at a precocious thirteen. She's been in love with kick butt heroines ever since.

With her overactive imagination, and channeling her inner Buffy, it was only a matter a time before she started creating her own characters. Waiting for her chance at a job as a ninja assassin, Nana, meantime works out her drama, passion and sass with fictional characters every bit as sassy and kick butt as she thinks she is.

nanamaloneromance.net

Made in the USA
Columbia, SC
30 January 2018